THIS WILDERNESS JOURNEY

THE MOUNTAIN SERIES ~ BOOK 7

MISTY M. BELLER

Misty M. Beller

BOOKS

ISBN-13 Trade Paperback: 978-0-9997012-3-2

ISBN-13 Large Print Paperback: 978-1-954810-37-2

ISBN-13 Casebound Hardback: 978-1-954810-38-9

To my own Hollow Oak.
Follow the dreams God has given you.
I'll be cheering you on!

How think ye? If a man have an hundred sheep, and one of them be gone astray, doth he not leave the ninety and nine, and goeth into the mountains, and seeketh that which is gone astray?

Matthew 18:12 (KJV)

CHAPTER 1

November, 1857
Canadian Rocky Mountains

I am the luckiest man alive. Here I stand at the edge of the world, nothing below me but rock and mountain and snow and a lake so clear it reflects the sky like green moss. It's not yet frozen, but I know it soon will be. Another wonder of God. The stack of His marvels so high it stretches as far as I can see.

And here I stand in the midst of them. A place as beautiful as heaven, surely.

So why do my eyes sting? Why does my heart ache?

What do I long for?

If I could form it with words, maybe then I would know what I seek. I could focus my restless energy on a goal. A single purpose that would make this life worth living.

How much longer can I live with this flood of emotion that churns through my mind and chest? How much longer can I withstand this saturation of feeling before I lose the ability to feel at all?

Maybe I am there already.

*J*oseph Malcom closed his leather journal and stared out at the view one last time. Snowcapped peaks stretching as far as he could see, rising into the heavens, some of them covered completely by clouds. Far below, scrawny pines and firs darkened the valleys, winding around and between the green pools that dotted the flat ground.

The wild beauty of this land had fascinated him since he'd first traveled into this country. The craving to explore these peaks had been part of what urged him to stay on here in these Canadian Rockies instead of returning to Baltimore—the only other place he could think of as home.

Even after the violence that had stripped away his wholeness, this landscape drew him still. His limp hand no longer throbbed, just hung without life. Useless.

The ache in his chest had changed. Shifted. Become more like a longing. An itch to keep moving. If he had to assign a word to the tightness in his chest, he just might call it…pain.

But that was silly, because he was happy out here. Even maimed, he was free to come and go anywhere he wanted. And he loved that freedom. Really.

With a sigh, he rose to his feet and stepped toward Copper. Joseph used his right hand to scoop up his rifle from the cave entrance and headed toward his gelding. The animal nibbled at tiny grass shoots but raised its head when Joseph neared.

After slipping the rifle in the scabbard tied to his saddle, he patted Copper's neck and strode around to the near side to mount. Once in the saddle, he scanned his campsite one last time to make sure he'd packed everything. The rocky cave opening no longer yawned dark and foreboding as it once had.

Now its murky depth seemed more like a welcoming hideaway. Home. Almost.

At the very least, a landing spot where he could come after each of his wanderings. Near enough to his sister's new cabin and the ranch in the valley below where his aunt and uncle raised their livestock.

But up here, he wasn't so near that he intruded on their privacy. With Emma still adjusting to her new family life, she needed to get her bearings without her twin brother hovering.

Or maybe the separation was for him. He didn't know anymore.

He steered Copper toward the trail. It'd been over a month since his last visit, so it was time to check in on them.

As the horse picked its way down the mountain, Joseph's gaze followed a path leading off to the right. It didn't look as if that trail had seen much traffic lately. The hot springs there weren't as large as the pools farther north where the nearby tribe of Peigan Blackfoot Indians preferred to visit. That suited Joseph just fine. Here, just a short ride from his cave, it felt almost as though the mineral water served as his private bath.

He ran a grimy hand over his equally grimy face. He probably should have availed himself of the pleasure before heading to see Em. He ducked his chin to sniff his shirt. Yes, that would have been the wiser choice.

The air seeped out of him, sagging his shoulders. He didn't have the energy to stop and unpack everything for a bath now. In truth, he itched to see Em again. And baby Hannah, and even Simeon. People.

No...they were more than that. They were his family. Though they didn't need him anymore, and no matter how much he tried to love the nomadic life he lived now, some days left an ache in his chest to return to the old days. Days when he could stop in to check on Emma any time he wanted. The days she relied on him.

He pushed Copper into a longer stride as the ground leveled off, and they skirted a patch of fir trees. He could stop for a second at the creek ahead. The water would be icy, but at least he could clean the worst of the trail dirt from his hands and face.

That way, Emma would let him play with his pudgy-cheeked niece. Maybe he'd give her his carved blocks today instead of waiting for her birthday next week. One year. It was hard to believe it had been only twelve months since he and his sister had arrived in Canada. That trip seemed like another lifetime. As if he'd always roamed these mountains, climbing rocky peaks just to see the view from the crest.

The water in the creek was as cold as he'd expected, and it roused his senses better than coffee used to, pumping blood so strong he could feel its thump without touching his neck. After using his good hand to swing back on Copper, he guided the gelding back to the trail.

Within moments, the little three-room cabin came into view, the door open wide and light filtering from inside. A horse stood tied to the front porch rail. A rail that hadn't been there on his last visit. Simeon must be keeping busy these days.

Joseph reined Copper to a stop in the yard and tied him a few paces away from the bay mare. "Hold tight, boy." He stroked the gelding, and Copper eased out a long sigh, dropping his head as if he planned to use the respite for a nap. Joseph patted the animal one last time on the rump, then he stepped away. He did the same to the mare, taking her measure as he passed. She was more gangly than Em's mare, and a little taller. He didn't recognize her from Uncle Adrien's stock, but she might be a new horse they were breaking in.

Voices drifted from the open door. Emma's laugh. A child's squeal. A deeper chuckle, but not rich enough to be Simeon's.

Joseph's senses jumped to alert, and he stopped inside the doorway to let his eyes adjust to the dimmer light.

"Joey!" A chair scraped, and the ruffle of Emma's skirts gave him enough warning to brace before his sister lunged into his arms.

He caught her, clinging with a grip almost as tight as the one she held on him. Something flipped in his chest, strengthening the longing. Em was like the other half of him. He'd stayed away much too long.

She drew back to study his face, her eyes seeking out more than he was ready to reveal. He looked past her, pushing aside her scrutiny. "Where's my niece hiding?"

"Ba!" A squeal from the table was accompanied by a banging on the wood. He smiled at the rosy face that grinned at her mother triumphantly. The child had some kind of muddy mixture spread across her cheeks and in her brown curls, not to mention on her hands, the spoon, and the table.

Another chair scraped, and Joseph pulled Emma aside so he could get a look at the person rising from the seat at the other end of the table.

"Joseph, you remember Father Bergeron." Emma kept a firm hold on his elbow as he stepped forward. "He's the missionary working with the Indian tribe in the next valley."

The tension in his shoulders eased as he took in the man's black collar and robes, the somber color broken only by the silver crucifix hanging from his neck, tucked into the cloth belting his waist.

Joseph extended his hand. "Father. Good to see you."

A touch of a smile softened the priest's leathered face. "Monsieur Malcom. You are always a blessing."

He couldn't help but raise his brows at that, but he held his tongue. A blessing didn't describe him much these days. Turning his focus on the imp sitting at the other end of the table, he descended on her. "And how's my little muffin? Are you good enough for Uncle Joey to eat?" He went in for a bite, using his whiskers to tickle her neck as she succumbed to giggles, tucking her chin and squirming away.

After a little more teasing, he straightened and turned back to the adults, focusing on Emma. "Where's Simeon?"

Emma stepped to the counter and poured from a pitcher. "He's helping Jock with the cattle today. Do you want a glass of milk?"

He grinned. "Milk? You are domestic these days."

She turned a sweet grin on him and extended the cup. "You could use some domestic."

That remark struck a bit close to home, but he kept his grin in place to disguise the hit.

The priest cleared his throat. "I am once again reminded of God's grace to his children, for in my prayers this morning, I mentioned how much I wished I might find you today."

The words were so unexpected, Joseph had to replay them in his head to make sure he'd heard correctly through the French accent. "You wanted to find me?" He hadn't meant for his voice to pitch high at the end, and it made him feel too much like a school boy.

The twinkle in the other man's dark gaze sparkled like the white of his hair. "I have a great favor to ask, and I can't think of a man more capable for the job."

"What's that." Something about the way those sparkling eyes regarded him made his neck itch. Or maybe he was afraid they could see into his soul. This man made a good priest with his love of the Scriptures, his gentle bearing, and that penetrating gaze. Did he see a hollowness where Joseph's soul should reside?

And where had that thought come from?

"My cousin is coming to help in my work," Father Bergeron said. "I sent word for Monty to ride with a freighter as far as Fort Hamilton and promised I would provide transportation from there." A frown deepened the lines on his forehead, and the twinkle faded from his eyes. "There is sickness with the tribe of Blood Indians, and I hate to leave them in this time of need. Just when they're beginning to open to me." Something like a sadness passed through his gaze, then it firmed to resolve. "But I can't leave Monty at the fort much longer either."

He fingered the cord holding the crucifix around his neck. "You're well-versed in the land around us. Would you be willing to bring my cousin the remaining distance to our camp?"

Joseph tilted his head, calculating what the request would involve. "You mean travel to Fort Hamilton?" That was a three-day trip at least. "When do you expect your cousin to be there?"

The priest's gaze squinted toward the open door as if he could see over the distance to determine when this Monty fellow would arrive. "I imagine Monty's already there waiting. It's been long enough." He turned back to Joseph, a plea on his kind face. "Would you be willing?"

And when a man of God looked at him like that, how could he decline? He raised a shoulder and glanced at Emma. "I suppose. Now is a good time to travel, before winter hits." A chill had already crept into the autumn air. Time was growing short before snow would come in earnest.

"God bless you." Father Bergeron stepped closer and took Joseph's good hand, clasping it in both of his.

The warmth of the human contact crept up Joseph's arm and

settled in his chest. His mouth even threatened to return the man's smile.

"My cousin's surname is Bergeron, as well. I sent word to Monsieur Hamilton requesting secure lodgings, so ask at the trading post. I'm sure they can direct you."

The man withdrew his hand and turned to Emma. "Now that my work here is accomplished, I need to get back."

In less than a minute they'd bid the priest farewell, and a strange quiet descended over the cabin.

Hannah squawked, and Emma stepped over to clean up the messy toddler. Joseph couldn't bring himself to move, as though his mind hung suspended mid-thought.

"Does that mean you're leaving right away?" Emma's quiet voice broke through his fog, and he turned to meet her gaze as she settled Hannah on the wooden floor.

He let out a breath and scrubbed a hand through his unruly hair. "I suppose so. It sounded like he's worried about his cousin staying too long at the fort." He scrunched his face. "I would be too with the reputation of the place."

She tipped her head. "It's bad?"

He squinted one eye at her. "Fort Whoop-up? Haven't you heard what the Blackfeet say about it?"

She raised both brows. "I don't meet as many people as you these days."

He snorted. The picture she painted was cock-eyed.

Then her face turned thoughtful. "While you're there, could you check on a shipment I ordered? It's possible it came with the freighter who brought Father Bergeron's cousin."

Joseph eyed her. "Sure. Anything special in it?" Something about the pink tinging her cheeks raised his curiosity.

"Maybe."

He drilled her with his gaze as she turned to wipe the table and chair. She could feel his question, he was pretty sure of it.

At last she peered up at him with a soft smile, the pink in her cheeks blooming wider. "I ordered a guitar for Simeon."

A darkness spread through his chest, rising up to cut off his air. "Why'd you do that? I gave him mine, remember?"

Her eyes turned gentle. "You'll want yours back, Joey."

His gut churned, and he ground his teeth as he fought to keep his voice low for the sake of the child playing on the rug. "I can't play it, Emma. I won't ever be able to play it." He held up his left hand, the useless fingers curling in scrawny, deformed balls. "Keep the guitar. I won't need it."

He spun and charged toward the door, the burn inside overcoming all his good intentions.

"Joseph." His sister's tone broke through the noise inside him. The sharp command in her voice pulling him to a stop. He could feel her intensity all the way to his core, but he didn't turn to face her.

"Joey, don't leave. Please. Stay and play with Hannah. She's missed you. We all have."

He let the air seep from his lungs, stealing his anger with it. His accident hadn't been Emma's fault. She shouldn't have to bear his temper. And he couldn't deny the longing in her tone. In truth, it connected with the yearning in his own chest. The bond of twins was a physical connection, soul deep.

Turning, he couldn't quite meet her eyes, but he stepped over to the rug and settled down beside his niece.

"You'll at least stay the night, won't you?"

He let his gaze roam Hannah's features as her finger stroked the soft rabbit fur that formed hair for her carved doll. "I'll leave in the morning." The words thickened the air between them, but not as dense as the weight they'd lodged in his chest.

Leaving shouldn't bother him anymore. It was a skill he'd honed this last year. He should be good at it by now.

⌒

Fort Hamilton felt like a city. There were half a dozen people visible in the open square as Joseph rode through the main gates. Two men in buckskins stood talking to an Indian brave beside a building along the perimeter wall. Blackfoot by the look of the man. Another trapper stood near them, watching the interaction as he stroked a long beard. Joseph headed that direction.

"Haloo, the fort." He halted Copper and the two pack horses trailing him, then slid to the ground in front of the man.

"Howdy."

Joseph paused to take in the man's grubby clothes and unkempt hair. Except for the heavy salting in his beard, Joseph probably looked just as bad. A glance down at his buckskins confirmed it. At least he'd stopped to wash his face and hands at the last river crossing. And he'd shaved before he left Emma's cabin, so he only had four days' growth on his face. Still, he'd have been tarred and feathered back in Texas if he'd let himself slip into this grubby unwashed state. But that had been another life.

Maybe once he found the priest's cousin, he could search out a place for a decent bath. At the very least, he could head back to that last river.

Joseph extended his good hand to the man, who took it with a shade of curiosity tinging his expression.

"I'm looking for a fellow by the name of Monty Bergeron. He probably arrived here with a freighter and is waiting for someone to take him the rest of the way to an Indian mission."

The trader's mouth twisted, and a strange light crept into his eyes. "Bergeron, you say? The only Bergeron I know's stayin' in that there corner hut." He motioned to the end of the row of buildings. "I'mma thinkin' he's not what yer expectin' though."

Joseph quirked a brow. He hadn't really formed an expectation. Maybe a gray-haired priest like Father Bergeron. "'Preciate the help." He started to turn away, then paused. "Is there a place a fella can pay for a bath around here? And maybe a laundry?"

The man sent a stream of dark liquid into the dirt between them. "River out back."

Ah...should have expected that, what with the appearance of this trader. "Much obliged."

He strolled along the row of buildings toward the end, pulling the horses with him. When he reached the corner structure, the door was open, but the dim interior made it hard to distinguish the view past the splash of sunlight on the threshold. He knocked on the frame. "Anyone home?"

Something rustled inside, like the sound of thick fabric. Had he awakened Mr. Bergeron? That didn't seem likely in the middle of the day, but maybe the man was much older than his cousin and had lain down for a nap. If that were the case, he wouldn't be a good fit to live in this wild country.

Footsteps came closer, along with the increased noise of the rustling fabric. Leaning forward, he peered inside as a figure stepped into the light streaming from outside. A flash of yellow pulled him back a step. Then his eyes focused on the image, his mind not quite believing what he saw.

A woman?

CHAPTER 2

So far have I come, I can scarcely recognize my old self.
~ Monti's Journal

onti Bergeron squared her shoulders and stepped forward to greet the man standing on her threshold. With the way the men at this fort all wore the same buckskin uniform —complete with thick beard and dirty hat—she couldn't tell for sure if she'd met this one before or not.

She raised her chin and forced a confident, yet pleasant, expression. *"Bonjour."*

He startled, his eyes growing as wide as the round hand mirror tucked in her trunk. Apparently, she wasn't whom he expected.

"May I help you, *monsieur?"*

He stroked his beard, which was shorter than the long scraggly hair the other men wore. His appearance might be a touch more groomed. And cleaner.

The amber brown of his eyes pierced her as confusion churned in their depths. "I…was looking for a Mister Bergeron. I must be at the wrong place. My apologies, ma'am." He reached up as if to tip a hat, but he wore nothing on his wavy mop of chestnut hair.

She allowed him a consolatory grin. Antoine must have forgotten to tell him the new missionary was a woman. It would be just like Papa's cousin to consider a detail like whether she was male or female irrelevant. After all, weren't all people loved equally by God?

The man started to turn away, so she spoke quickly. "You seek Monti Bergeron?"

He looked back. "Yes, ma'am. Do you know him?"

She raised her jaw another notch. "I am Mademoiselle Monti Bergeron."

He nodded, a polite gesture. "Hello, ma'am. I didn't realize he was married. Father Bergeron sent me to take you and your husband the rest of the way. Is he around? Your husband, I mean."

She pursed her lips against a smile. The man apparently didn't know his French well enough to understand that Mademoiselle meant she was *not* married. "You misunderstand, Monsieur. I am Monticello Bergeron. My family prefers to call me Monti. I am the new missionary."

If his eyes had been wide before, they grew round as plates now. Then narrowed. His head cocked.

She held her tongue, waiting. But the silence stretched farther.

Finally, "You?"

Was the man dim-witted? Or had it been so long since he'd seen a female? She fit a hand at her waist. "*Oui*. When should I be ready to depart?"

He straightened as if he were trying to pull himself together. "You are Father Bergeron's cousin then?"

Now he was becoming irritating. "Oui. Of course." She glanced behind him to the horses standing with heads drooping. "I can be ready to leave in a half hour. Will we be traveling by wagon?"

She could endure a few more days riding in the same kind of rough wooden structure that carried her the last few weeks. But it would be a relief to finally settle in at the mission.

The man's eyes dimmed, and he seemed to close up a little. "We'll be on horseback. I've some trading to do, and the horses need a rest. We'll leave out at first light."

Horseback? A wave of concern swept through her chest, and she stepped forward as he started to turn away. "Monsieur."

He stalled, then looked at her with brows lifted.

"Will my trunk fit on the horse's back?" She'd consolidated all her belongings into one trunk when she'd first joined up with the freighter back in Fort Walsh. But everything in that box was essential. Bibles and other writings to help their ministry to the Indians. Her clothing and personal items. Pictures of Papa and Mama. She'd let go of everything else, but these... These precious mementos she would not part with. All she had left of her family. Everything except God and a cousin she'd not seen in fifteen years.

The mountain man eyed her with a dubious expression. "No, ma'am. The trunk won't fit on the horse's back." The tone of his voice rose with the last sentence, almost as if he mimicked her words.

Her hackles flared. "Then how do you propose we carry my trunk?" She would give him the opportunity to work it out himself before she demanded he hire a wagon.

His gaze ran over her—not indecently, but as if he were trying to calculate something. Maybe how much room she'd take up? Then he turned to eye the three horses behind him. "I brought the bay mare for you to ride. I need the pack horse for supplies. I suppose I might be able to trade for another horse to carry your things. It'd be a sight easier if you could tie 'em in bundles instead of a trunk, though." He turned back to face her then, his hand coming up to rub his beard. "You sure Father Bergeron knows you're a lady?"

The statement was so ludicrous she probably should have been offended, but the slightly bewildered honesty with which he spoke... she couldn't help the laugh that popped out. It rubbed her funny bone as it escaped, and she couldn't contain the mirth.

He tilted his head at her, one corner of his mouth quirking up as if she were an oddity he couldn't decipher.

The sight only increased her giggles, and she grabbed at her waist and fought to get ahold of herself. Maybe it was the stress of the long journey or the two expectant weeks she'd waited here for Antoine, but her shoulders shook, and she doubled over with uncontrollable laughter. Tears stung her eyes, and she finally released herself to the emotions bubbling inside her, freeing herself to let the mirth flow.

At last, she struggled to catch her breath, wiping away the tears that trailed down her cheeks. *"Excusez moi."* She gasped for air and sniffed, forcing herself to meet the man's gaze. His eyes had softened, a bit of cautious pleasure in their depths. Not the scorn she'd been afraid she'd find there.

Pressing a hand to her chest, she exhaled a long breath. "I am sorry. You must be wondering what kind of unbalanced female you've been settled with. I assure you, I'm not so unstable, I just..." She waved a hand, searching for the right words. "It's just been..." Oh, pity.

Sniffing, she pressed both hands to smooth her skirts, then cleared her throat. "Anyway. Monsieur..." She paused. "What did you say your name was?"

He raised a brow, still eyeing her as though she might turn into a horse before him at any moment. "Joseph. Joseph Malcom."

"Well, Monsieur Malcom. I've consolidated all I own to one trunk. I would be thankful if we could find a way to transport my things." She offered a smile as a sort of truce. The fit of laughter had released tension she hadn't realized she carried. And now, her heart went out to this frontiersman. He'd thought he was coming to pick-up a man and had planned the transportation accordingly. The least she could do was work with him to find an alternate solution.

He nodded. "I'll see what's available." Then he turned away again, but paused for the second time and looked back. "Can you be ready to head out first thing in the morning? I'll come for you at first light."

She dipped a curtsey. "I'll be ready."

~

*A*s Joseph led the horses toward the trading post store—away from Miss Bergeron's scrutiny—his mind still struggled to catch up. He'd been sent here to pick-up a *woman*? How could he have missed that detail?

He replayed Father Bergeron's words in his head and couldn't remember anything that would have tipped him off one way or the other. He'd just assumed.

But why? Why would an elegant young woman like the one he'd just met come out to this wilderness? And to preach to the Indians? Bile churned in his gut. He didn't want to imagine all the ways that could end. What had possessed her to come this far? And unprotected? It was a wonder she'd survived here at the trading post without a guardian. What had her family been thinking to allow her to come?

No matter what the reason, a young woman on her own clearly didn't belong in this brutal wilderness. Did Father Bergeron plan to take her into the Indian camps? How did he expect to protect her? As far as Joseph knew, the priest didn't even own a gun.

Joseph tied the horses to the rail in front of the trading post, then stalked inside. For now, the woman was his responsibility. Her and that trunk he was supposed to find a way to tote.

But when he'd finished bartering for a fourth horse and supplies to trade with the Indians, he couldn't help but ask the old trader, "So how long has Miss Bergeron been staying at the fort?" He stacked a bag of cornmeal on top of his pile, careful not to make eye contact with the man.

"Purty thing, ain't she?"

Joseph didn't look up or agree with the old timer. Her beauty had almost overwhelmed him, especially in that yellow dress, but discussing it with this fellow wouldn't do her any favors. In fact, the more they could keep her from sticking out like a tree in the middle of a meadow, the better chance he had of keeping her alive and unsullied out here in this wild country full of even wilder men.

He pinched his mouth. Should he ask her to wear something a

little less…flattering while they were on the trail? That bright yellow would stand out for five hundred yards. But probably, they wouldn't run into anyone once they got out of town.

It was likely she'd need better clothes once she was in the Indian camp. Buckskins would be the best thing, like the squaws wore. Although he couldn't envision the French princess he'd just met wearing buckskin. He glanced toward the stack of cloth on one of the shelves. Brown was the only color there. Should he purchase some for her to make up a new dress? Would she be insulted by the idea? It shouldn't matter as long as it kept her alive and safe. He pursed his lips. How much would he even buy?

Striding toward the material, he lifted a folded piece from the top. The heavy stuff formed a sturdy handful. Turning back, he carried it to the pile. "Add this to the tally."

~

*M*onti was ready when the knock came the next morning. She set her mug on the table and rose from her chair. When she pulled open the door, the sight that greeted her was not quite what she'd expected.

Monsieur Malcom stood with a cluster of horses behind him. Yet he looked nothing like she remembered from yesterday. In the dim light of early morning, his clean-shaven face nearly sparkled. His skin was a healthy bronze, even where the beard had been, giving proof to the fact that the overgrowth he'd worn so comfortably yesterday was not his usual mien.

And his shaven face only added to the intensity of his amber eyes and the brown lashes framing them. He stared at her, those eyes scrutinizing. His Adam's apple bobbed as he swallowed. A hat dangled from his hand, and the crease in his damp hair meant he'd doffed it for her. At least he'd shown decent manners thus far.

The thought of traveling alone with this man for the final leg of her journey had coiled her stomach in a knot all morning, but surely Antoine would have sent someone trustworthy. Right? Her cousin tended to look for the good in everyone. But Mama had always trusted him implicitly, which meant surely Antoine would have ensured the honor of anyone he'd sent to retrieve her.

She had to believe that. Although, if this man did prove less than honorable, she could handle that as well. In addition to the handgun affixed under her skirts, she'd been thoroughly trained in the oriental arts of self-defense, ever since the night of her fifteenth birthday.

Men, she could handle.

"Bonjour." She dipped a slight curtsey, then stepped back and motioned to the trunk she'd dragged beside the door. "I am ready, as you see."

His gaze pulled from her to the box, and a line creased his brow. "We'll have to unpack it."

She nodded and stepped forward to open the lid. She'd expected as much, which was why she'd tied her possessions in tight bundles inside.

The man retreated to one of the horses, then returned with an oil cloth. He knelt beside the trunk and started wrapping the bundles in the waterproof material. There was something about the way he handled each. His motions weren't awkward exactly, but he seemed to use his left hand in an odd way.

Or…as she studied his motions, it seemed like he didn't actually use that hand at all. Just the wrist and arm to brace things as he wrapped the oil cloth around her belongings. Did his gloves conceal an injury?

He glanced up at her and caught her staring.

She averted her gaze and strode to the table. "I've packed a few tidbits for us to eat as we travel. I assumed you've planned meals for us, or should I purchase food before we leave?"

"I have food." He almost grunted the words, then pushed to his feet and carried her things out to the animals.

There was nothing left to do but stand and watch as he secured her belongings onto the pack saddle of a brown horse. The saddle was really more of a platform, and her bundles heaped higher and higher as he tied them on. His broad shoulders shifted as he moved, drawing

17

her eyes to the ropy muscles just visible above the edge of his buck-skin collar. From the thickness of his chest, that muscle was only a small sample of what lay beneath.

She ripped her gaze away. What was she doing imagining such things? She glanced around the little fort, the sight that had worn at her weary nerves for days now. Suddenly, this tiny village of dirty, bearded traders felt like home. Familiar. The men had been respectful, if a bit uncouth.

And now she was leaving. Heading out into the unknown wilderness with a man she'd hardly spent more than a quarter hour with. Had she taken leave of her senses?

Fear not, for I have redeemed you; I have called you by your name; you are Mine. The words whispered into her thoughts, lacing themselves through her chest, relaxing the knot in her stomach. God had called her to this place. He had planned this trip long before the idea took root in her mind. And He had work for her at her destination. His work.

When you walk through the fire, you shall not be burned, nor shall the flame scorch you. Those words from Isaiah had held her together after her fifteenth birthday, and every other moment since, when fear tried to nip at her resolve. She'd clung to them more than once on this arduous journey. Now, she'd almost reached her destination, and then her work would truly begin.

"That should do it."

She jumped at the voice that pulled her from her reverie.

Monsieur Malcom spared her only a quick glance as he left the pack horse and stepped to the animal at the front of the line. Then he turned to face her directly, scrutiny narrowing his eyes. "I'd planned for this mare to be yours. I'm still not sure I should take you into the wilderness country. It won't be anything like you're used to. No stores or ready-made anything. And between the animals and the elements, there's a good chance you won't live past your first year. Would you rather turn back?"

The question was enough to slough off the last of her mental wanderings. She narrowed her gaze at him. "Of course I'd rather not turn back." Raising her chin, she strode forward, focusing on the saddle—not the man watching her every movement. Under his scrutiny, it would be harder than she'd anticipated to keep from revealing that she'd never ridden a horse before.

Stopping in front of the animal, she surveyed the leather contraption. "How do I get on?"

He moved beside the horse's side and dropped to one knee, cupping his hands in front of him. "I'll boost you up."

Was she supposed to put her foot in his hands? Her knee? No, letting him touch her leg was out of the question. Gingerly, she stepped into his grip, then grabbed onto the leathers and started to climb. It was an awkward business, more so than she'd expected from watching the men in this fort step aboard their horses so effortlessly. The ruffles of her skirts didn't help the matter either.

Using every bit of the strength in her arms, she finally hauled herself into the saddle, then grabbed onto the handle in front while she tried to make the world right itself around her. The height of this beast was almost dizzying. It hadn't looked so tall from the ground.

As the frantic pace of her heart slowed, she forced herself to look at the man, pasting on a confident smile. "Ready when you are."

He studied her with an enigmatic expression. Scrutinizing. Wary.

She held the smile as firmly as she could, but it wavered a bit under his intensity.

Then he finally turned to pat the mare. He picked up the leather straps that rested on the horse's neck and held them up to Monti. "Use these reins to steer her. Pull right to turn right, left to go left. Tug straight back to stop. To make the horse go, squeeze her with your… um…around her girth area." His gaze flicked to her legs, and heat crept unbidden up Monti's neck. At least he had the decency not to name parts of her person.

She took the reins in one hand, keeping the other clamped around the saddle's handle. "I'm ready."

CHAPTER 3

I'll never understand this life that's been thrust upon me.
~ Joseph's Journal

*A*nother surprise. Could she be *less* prepared for life in the wilderness? Every interaction with this French princess handed out something new.

Joseph swung aboard Copper and checked the strap that tethered his to the first pack horse. Everything secure. He glanced back at the woman mounted on the horse behind him. She did a decent job of masking her apprehension, but the way she clutched the saddle proved she was more than a little nervous. How had she never ridden a horse before? It was almost inconceivable. She must truly be a princess, must have been sheltered away in a French castle somewhere, safeguarded from the need to learn skills her serfs would consider critical to survival.

So, what was she doing out here in the Canadian wilderness? No wonder she'd seemed surprised when he hadn't had a wagon. She didn't belong out here any more than the King of England.

Turning Copper around, he eyed the woman, then spoke the words he should have said when he first met her. "You need to go back home, Miss Bergeron. The mountain country is no place for a lady. I'll arrange a ride back east for you, or I'll take you myself."

She straightened a good six inches, every hint of nerves replaced with the pluck of a mama hen protecting her brood from a skulking dog. "I will not, Monsieur, I assure you."

He glared back at her. "You will, ma'am. I don't think the priest knew exactly what he was agreeing to when he said you could come out here. It's not safe, and I won't be a party to it. I'll find you a safe ride, and you can go back to your family."

"I have no family." She fairly spat the words in her French cadence. "My papa is dead. My mama, as well. There is nothing for me to return to. So, Monsieur Malcom, I will go to serve with Antoine, and you may assist me in my journey or not. But I warn you—do not stand in my way."

The fierceness in her gaze made him—just for a moment—want to sidle back away from her. Although he barely knew this woman, he had no doubt she'd do exactly what she'd said. After all, she'd come this far on her own. He had no idea where she'd traveled from, but the place had to be weeks away, at least. She might have been exposed to men of all sorts in her journey so far, but she'd probably not experienced the wild animals and fierceness of nature she'd meet on the final stretch of her journey.

He couldn't let her face that alone.

Narrowing his gaze at her, he met those eyes that still sparked with anger. "I'll take you. But let me be clear, Miss Bergeron. The country we're about to face is no trifling matter. To survive, I expect you to do exactly as I say, when I say it. Do we have an agreement?"

She nodded—a single curt dip of her chin. "I will do as you say."

He let out a breath, studying her one final moment. He should be hanged for even thinking about taking her into this wilderness. But it didn't look as if he had a choice.

"*W*hat's my horse's name?"

Joseph straightened at the lilting accent of the delicate voice behind him. A small part of him wanted to learn more about her, but he wasn't accustomed to conversation breaking the silence on the trail. Maybe he could handle a question or two, though. Silence left him alone with his thoughts, and that too often sent him in a downward spiral of melancholy.

"Doesn't have a name. At least I don't think so. She's part of my uncle's stock. One of the breeders."

"I think I'll call her Velvet. Her fur is so soft here on her shoulder."

He kept his focus straight forward. "With horses, they call it hair."

"Her hair is so soft on her shoulder." A hint of mirth touched her voice. At least that was what it sounded like. The way her accent lifted each word made them tinkle in the air like the clear tones of a bell. He could easily get sucked into their cadence. He'd have to guard against that.

Silence settled back over them as the trail rose up a gently rolling hill, and Joseph let the sounds of the grassland weave their way through him. The coo of a mourning dove called in the distance, and a breeze swept across his neck. It was good he'd let Emma give him a trim before he started out on this journey. The French princess probably thought him enough of a barbarian as he was.

"I confess, I thought there would be more mountains, from the way my cousin described this country in his letters."

Joseph swept a glance at the gentle swells around them. "We'll get to the peaks. Have about a day's ride in this part of the country, then we'll reach the foothills. After that, the mountains."

"How far away is the mission?" Her tone sounded surprised, but that might have been only the lift of her accent.

"About three days." Although if she wasn't used to riding, they might need to take it slower, with shorter days in the saddle. "Or more, possibly. Depending on how far we travel each day."

Silence eased over them again, and Joseph was just settling into it when the bright voice sounded again.

"Do you know my cousin well, Monsieur Malcom?"

Did she plan to talk the entire way? He cleared his throat and adjusted the brim of his hat. "Call me Joseph. We're not so fancy out here." She may as well get that settled in her pretty head. "And I've known Father Bergeron for about a year, off and on. He seems like a fine man. He's doing well with the Indians, I hear, although he's got his work cut out for him."

"What can you tell me about the Peigan tribe? That's their name, right?" An excitement entered her voice, as if she were eager for news of home not of a tribe of natives.

"Well." He measured his words. "This particular band stays at the edge of the mountain country, where they have good access to water. They keep to themselves pretty well, not really fighting with the other tribes."

"Have any been converted to faith in Christ?"

He gripped his reins tighter. "I couldn't say, ma'am."

That must have satisfied her, because she let the silence take over again.

But this time, he didn't let it immerse him. She would break the quiet soon, so he might as well keep himself from getting lost in his thoughts.

Except she didn't speak. And the longer he waited for it, the more tension tightened his shoulders. Maybe this was a good time to ask some of his own questions.

"So...Monti. That's not usually a girl's name, is it?" Let her think him impertinent. That name was the source of all his confusion over her gender, which surely gave him the right to ask about it.

"My father loved great French architecture, and he saw Mr. Jefferson's Monticello plantation on a business trip right before I was born. Mama said it was all he spoke of for weeks."

Joseph turned to study her over his shoulder, easing back on Copper's reins to slow the gelding until they rode side by side. "Your father named you after Thomas Jefferson's home?"

This dainty princess had been named after a building? Sure it had been a majestic structure, but still... What father would name his daughter such? She should have been Rose or Camille—some name befitting an elegant French flower.

She gave a half-shrug, and her gaze wandered to her hands. "It was something he loved, I suppose. My papa was…unique." She looked up then and met his gaze. "Eccentric, some said."

She'd said her father was dead, but the tone in her voice didn't sound like fresh mourning. Didn't really sound like grief at all. Sort of like longing.

"You must have been dear to him."

She held his gaze, despite the jostling from the rolling gate of her horse. "Maybe." The word wasn't much more than a breath, and she looked away, out over the low valley and the swell of the next hill.

"How old were you when he died?"

"Five." She said it without preamble. "I don't remember much of him anymore, but I do have a memory of touching his moustache. He would hold me on his knee and laugh so big his belly would bounce. I remember his laugh." Her voice faded with the last sentence, as though the reminiscence swallowed her up.

"A laugh is a good thing to remember. I can't think of a time my father laughed. Not like that."

She studied him, and Joseph looked away. Why had he brought up his own past? He'd only wanted to discover the reason behind her unusual name. He'd not planned it to turn into this…deeper sharing.

"Your father lives near your home here?"

Joseph shook his head, focusing on the line where the grassland met the horizon so he didn't have to look at Miss Bergeron. "He's buried in Texas with my mother." Something brown took shape in the distance. "Look, there's a deer."

She followed the line of his finger and made a little cooing sound. It drew his gaze to her face, where her delicate lips formed a soft bow. She was exquisite. Every bit of her looked like French royalty. Yet, the longing in her tone when she'd spoken of her father gave him the feeling her story wasn't exactly a fairytale.

More deer came into view as they drew closer. But the animals must have heard them, for they jerked their heads from the grass, then leapt away.

Silence took over again, although not a true quiet. The covey of doves that landed in the distance, the faraway cry of a whooping crane, and the steady blow of the wind that had grown as the day progressed helped him settle into the natural rhythm that soothed his nerves. And riding beside Miss Bergeron didn't seem quite so foreign as it had only hours ago.

They didn't share much conversation the rest of the morning, except for the times he pointed out an animal or some unique feature of the land. She seemed to soak it all in, as though hungry for each detail. Not the spoiled snob he'd suspected when he first met her yesterday.

He stopped them early for lunch at a stand of lodge pole pines. They'd not paused at all before that, and nature was calling him in a most persistent way. Besides, she would likely be sore after so many hours in the saddle. She'd appreciate a chance to stretch her legs.

After slipping from Copper, he strode around to assist her down. She looked a little uncertain, and he gripped the mare's reins. "Just move your right...um...foot behind you, then lean forward over the saddle and slide down."

She darted a warning glance at him, those dark brows arcing. He'd only said *foot*. She didn't have to wear a look as though she suspected he'd planned to touch her bare leg.

He narrowed his eyes back at her, trying to push down the sudden images his mind formed of him carrying out that last thought. "My apologies, Miss Bergeron. But if you haven't noticed, we're not in a ballroom."

Those expressive brown eyes narrowed, mirroring his look. But she didn't say anything, just straightened her ruffly blue skirt and obeyed the directions he'd given.

When she landed on the ground, she stumbled back a step. He steadied her with a hand on her shoulder, but the moment she stopped wobbling, she spun to face him, jerking from his touch.

He took his own step back and almost raised his hand to shield himself from the vehemence sparking in her eyes.

"You will keep your hands to yourself, Monsieur. Do I make myself clear?" She spit each word like an angry cougar, and he took another step back.

"Of course. Sorry for trying to help." He turned away, more to get away from the arrows in her glare than anything. Surely his assistance didn't merit this level of anger.

He stretched his lanky legs into long strides as he moved deeper into the patch of trees. She could fend for herself if she wished it.

~

*M*onti dragged in deep breaths as she struggled to steady her ragged pulse. She'd not meant to display that spurt of anger, but the pressure of his touch had loosened a fear that still coursed through her veins. She should have known better than to let herself travel alone with a man. The week she'd spent with the freighters had been different, but at least Mrs. Holland had been with them.

Out here, alone in this barren country with a man... He'd not meant anything by his touch, she was fairly sure of that from the flash of confusion in his eyes before they dimmed in anger. It didn't matter though. There was a reason she now required the strictest level of propriety from her male acquaintance. She would never, ever let that barrier down again.

It seemed her anger had set him straight. She could hope so anyway. She took a step forward. Needles shot through her ankles, and a steady burn started in her calves, working its way up her legs and into her lower back. Who would have thought riding horseback would be so painful?

By the time she'd paced two laps along the edge of the trees, her muscles were easing and Joseph reappeared from the woods.

He didn't look at her but headed straight for his horse and rummaged in the pack. Hopefully, he'd brought something substantial for their midday meal. She'd not expected the morning ride to make her so hungry.

And then another thought stilled her. Would he expect her to prepare the food? After all, when a cook couldn't be employed, that role was the woman's duty, wasn't it? Surely she could muddle through whatever had to be done.

"About lunch…" She took a tentative step toward him, but the man pulled a bundle out of his pack and turned to face her.

"I had Cookie make sandwiches so we could get back on the trail." He opened the leather wrapping and held it out to her. Two sandwiches sat on the leather as though on a serving tray.

She took one and eyed him. He'd still not met her gaze, and his manner was stiff, as though he'd rather be anywhere than conversing with her.

"*Merci*."

He nodded and turned away, still not looking at her.

She bit into the sandwich as he strode toward the horses with his own. The food was a bit dry but more than enough to sustain her through the remainder of the day. She should be thankful she'd not had to put the meal together. Yet, part of her felt almost affronted. Had he assumed she wasn't capable of preparing the food, so he'd purchased the meal ready-made? She could have handled it. She could accomplish anything she set her mind to.

Perhaps tonight, she would have the chance to prove that to him.

CHAPTER 4

*Once again, God has brought me to the place I least expect. Yet He must
believe I can handle it. I shall not let Him down.*
~ Monti's Journal

*S*urely, he'd not forgotten the biscuits.

Joseph rifled through the bundle of food supplies on the
new pack horse's back, but the leather-wrapped parcel wasn't there.
He'd paid half a month's wages for this ready-made food back at the
fort so Miss Bergeron wouldn't have to eat his gruel for two meals a
day. But somehow, he'd either misplaced the bundle or left it behind.

He had the dried venison pulled out already, and the cornmeal was
easy to access. Looked like mush it would be. She might as well get
used to the simple fare they ate in the mountains.

The only halfway-fancy meals she'd get would be from his sister,
Emma. She'd become a pretty decent cook this past year, and her food
was as tasty as anything they'd eaten back east. But then, she had
Simeon's hunting, and her garden, and a real cookstove Simeon had
hauled hundreds of miles for her.

After gathering enough wood, Joseph knelt to start the fire, using the wrist of his injured arm to help move the largest logs into place. The burn of Miss Bergeron's gaze seemed to pierce the glove protecting his useless hand. His skin itched under the leather, but he didn't dare rub it. Did she have to stand there and watch him?

He'd prepared the tinder and was ready to strike the flint, but she still hadn't moved. He sat back on his heels, barely suppressing a glare. Instead, he nodded toward the packs of food. "There's cornmeal in the leather sack. If you'll fetch a pan of water from the creek, you can mix up a mush. I'll have the fire ready to heat everything shortly."

She moved to do his bidding, the rustle of her skirts an odd sound mixed with the call of a distant whip-poor-will. While he coaxed a spark to catch on the tinder, he couldn't help the way the edges of his vision tracked her to the stream flowing a dozen strides away from their camp. Even with all his practice starting campfires, he was still so clumsy without the use of his left hand. Thankfully, she kept her focus on the ground ahead of her as she carried the pot of water back to the supplies.

"How much cornmeal should I add to the water?"

A spark landed on the tinder, and he knelt low to blow a gentle stream of air toward it. The light grew and finally broke into a tiny flame. He added another small breath, and the flame increased. When he paused to let the fire take hold on its own, he glanced over at Miss Bergeron. "Just enough to make a paste."

Over the next few minutes, he was able to coax the flame into a fire, and he sat back on his heels and looked around.

Miss Bergeron stood watching him, the cast iron pot in her hands and an uncertain expression on her face. "Here you go."

He took the pot and glanced inside. Clear water swam around the edges, while lumps of cornmeal seemed to weigh down the center. Apparently, she hadn't thought it necessary to mix the two. There was far too much water, also. When he added more cornmeal to get the mixture right, there'd be enough for the evening meal, and tomorrow morning, besides.

He slid a look at her. "You must be hungry."

A blush crept into her cheeks, and he turned away from the sight. She'd obviously never cooked corn mush. Which wasn't surprising, since she probably came from a high falutin' house where they employed a cook. He'd have to give better instructions next time.

Carrying the pot back to the food pack, he added more meal and stirred the mixture, then set it to heat in the fire. Now, he had a good bit of work to do settling the horses and making camp.

With a glance back at Miss Bergeron, he motioned toward the pot. "Keep an eye on the food. When it's warm, you can eat."

No need for her to wait for him. Hopefully, she'd keep from scalding it before he finished for the night.

~

*S*he'd burned the paste.

Monti held her breath against the acrid odor as she let the crude wooden spoon fall back against the rim of the pot. She was starving, but it would take strong willpower to keep this stuff down. She toed the heavy dish farther away from the fire.

Glancing around into the darkness outside the perimeter of firelight, she pulled her coat tighter around herself and tried to decipher what each foreign sound might be.

Joseph had been moving to and fro between the campsite and horses for a while, but as darkness settled securely—bringing with it a bone-chilling cold—he'd stayed out with the animals. Only the steady rustle of movement and occasional horse sound broke the eerie quiet of the night. What was he doing for so long out there? Avoiding her presence?

His behavior had bordered on brusque all afternoon, almost irritable. Or maybe that was her imagination, but he'd definitely not been talkative or easygoing like she would have expected after riding together all day. And although he'd not said as much, she could tell she'd failed at her attempt to make the cornmeal paste, or whatever this food was supposed to be.

But how could she be expected to complete the task well when she'd barely been given any guidance? The one instruction he had said to her—to eat without him—she'd not obeyed. After all, they might be in the middle of the western wilderness, but she didn't need to forsake all her manners. But if he didn't return soon, she might just follow his order. Her midsection had been making unseemly noises for what felt like hours.

At long last, a figure emerged from the shadows. She jumped at his sudden appearance, but as Joseph's face came into the light, she let out a long breath.

He plopped a stack of blankets on the ground, then turned to scan her and the fire.

She tried not to look eager as she motioned toward the pot. "I've been keeping the meal warm."

He nodded, then turned back to the blankets and started spreading them out.

"Are there bowls and spoons somewhere? I didn't see any in the food satchel."

"Don't usually bother with them."

Monti tried not to show her surprise, although he wouldn't have seen it with his back to her. "Do you plan for us to eat directly from the pot?" Using what? A common serving spoon? Their hands?

She knew he was a mountain man, but for some reason, she'd not expected him to be...crude. Or at least she'd not thought he'd expect it of her. Traveling with the freighters, Mrs. Holland had handled the cooking and provided basic serving ware.

Here, it seemed she'd have to fend for herself.

She moved to the pot and knelt beside it. "I suppose if we're to share utensils, I'd best speak a prayer over the food and start eating."

That finally brought his attention around to her. "I told you to do that already."

She didn't grace him with a look. "I thought to be polite and wait for you. I see now that manners were unnecessary."

It might be her imagination, but it sounded as if he growled as he turned back to his work.

~

"Joseph. Wake up."

Joseph forced his eyes open as the voice registered. A rustle of movement sounded near him, and he bolted upright, reaching for the rifle beside him.

Miss Bergeron. Her worried face was just visible in the shadows of the fading campfire.

"What's wrong?"

She wrapped a fur tighter around her. "I heard something howling. I think it might have been wolves."

He set the rifle down, then reached for a log from the stack he'd gathered. After settling it on the fire, he added a second and a third. "How far away did they sound?" She probably had heard wolves, but the horses weren't snorting or making restless sounds, so the predators must not be near enough to worry over.

"Close enough to wake me up."

Before he could respond, a howl sounded. Distant, but not so far that he could go back to sleep without a care.

"I think that was louder." Miss Bergeron's hushed voice seemed to echo in the silence following the wolf's cry.

They must be coming closer. If the animals were on the hunt, that was likely the last time they'd howl.

He tossed another log in the flames. "The fire will keep them away. Nothing to worry about." At this rate, though, he'd need to hunt for more wood as soon as dawn arrived so they could heat food for breakfast.

Then a thought filtered through his mind. One that instantly brought a surge of longing, then a swift stab of bitterness. Simeon's guitar. He'd carefully placed it atop the packs. The sound of a guitar would keep the wolves well away.

But with no feeling at all in the fingers of his left hand, the only sounds he could make would be rough, off-tune strumming. Although maybe he could play an easy chord or two if he used the heel of his left palm to hold down the strings. Perhaps.

In truth, the idea started a craving he could feel all the way to the tips of his fingers. Even in the lifeless fingers of his left hand. Like the phantom pain experienced by those who'd lost a limb, he could feel the yearning in his useless digits.

He glanced at his guest, who'd lain back down amongst her blankets and furs. The light flickered off her wide-open eyes as she stared at him. He settled himself against the tree beside his bedroll, keeping the rifle across his lap. "Go back to sleep, Miss Bergeron. I'll watch for a while and make sure there's nothing to be concerned about."

She nodded and closed her eyes. He waited several minutes as her eyelids occasionally flickered open to watch the flames dance in the fire. Then they would drift closed again, only to repeat the pattern a minute later. The chance to watch her, even across the distance the fire created, was a pleasure he shouldn't enjoy so much. She was such a beauty, with each delicate feature proportioned perfectly. Her skin seemed as creamy as fine china. Completely unmarred.

At last, her eyes stayed shut, and her perfectly formed lips parted to allow the steady breathing of sleep. He let a few more minutes pass, then eased up from his pallet and crept into the darkness.

The wooden guitar case sat exactly where he'd left it, and he cradled it as he crept back into the ring of firelight. He tried to position himself so the sound would drift away from Miss Bergeron, but he still had to make sure he had enough light to see the frets and strings.

He had to remove both gloves, and the night air pricked at his skin. His first attempt at an A chord was off-key, although close enough that the correct notes were discernable. Working his good hand between the strings and the knobs, he tuned the guitar, letting the familiar sound of each string soothe the knot in his chest.

At last he had them right and strummed once over the loose strings, producing the usual discordant sound. Even that familiar noise eased the muscles through his shoulders. It had been far too long since he'd wrapped himself around a guitar. Felt the music through the wooden body and into his soul.

He worked his hand back between the frets and formed the A

again. A little better. He worked at it more, transitioning into an E chord. He picked out an easy melody with his good hand while he tried to form some portion of the chords with the side and base of his left hand. Twisting the limb was awkward, but it seemed he was always bending into unnatural positions as he compensated for the limp fingers.

There was so much he had to compensate for. All because of that one horrendous day on the mountain. And the icy patch that had nearly been the death of him.

Some days he almost wished the rocks and snow had finished him off. But here, with the faint aroma of balsam wood drifting up to him, his good fingers resting on the strings... In this moment, a small part of his old self seemed to seep back in.

He bent over the guitar, letting his head hang limp as he focused on breathing. Feeling. Inhaling the memories of a life he could barely remember.

~

*M*onti eased her eyes open, barely daring to breathe. The sound of Joseph's movements had stilled for several minutes now. She had to know what he was doing.

As her vision focused on his form, she saw that he was bent over the guitar. His shoulders rose and fell with each deep breath. Had he fallen asleep?

As quietly as she could, she pushed upright and moved the blankets aside. Should she whisper his name to wake him again? If he was this exhausted, she probably should let him sleep as long as there was no danger lurking nearby. They'd not heard the wolves again, so that threat seemed to have passed. If he slept in the slumped over position the rest of the night, though, he'd awaken with all manner of aches.

She crept toward him, although what she planned to do exactly, she wasn't sure. Wake him, maybe? Perhaps extract the guitar from his clutch so he could relax. She stopped in front of him, taking in the strong shoulders that had slumped forward. His entire body seemed to rise with each breath. His left arm draped over the neck of the guitar, his hand dangling in his utterly relaxed state.

She reached for that arm to move it off as she began to extricate him. Something caught her gaze though. The hand glared white in the moonlight, as if it didn't often see the sun. Not an unlikely thought in this cold land where he probably wore gloves most of the time.

But what snagged her notice was the jagged red line running across the back of his hand from one side to the other. A scar? The wound must have been recent, at least within the past year, for the angry line glared up against the white of his skin. Skin that had probably been concealed in a bandage for weeks following this injury.

Reaching forward again, she took the hand in her own, stroking the red with her thumb. His fingers seemed more slender than she'd expected, perhaps from lack of use as he allowed the hand to heal.

As gently as she could, she rested his hand on the blanket beside him, then turned to focus on the rest of him. The guitar seemed to be supporting much of his weight, so she eased him sideways onto the blanket as she slid the instrument away.

Wonder of wonders, he didn't seem to awaken during any of the shifting. His breathing stilled when his head sank onto the blanket, but then he shifted to a more comfortable position, and the steady breaths came in regular succession again.

Only then did she begin breathing again, too. She took up the guitar and studied the instrument. It was much bigger than her violin, but the coarseness of the strings and the smooth grain of the wood made her long for the feel of her old friend. She was tempted to play a few chords, but she didn't dare wake Joseph. Besides, it wouldn't be the same.

Easing away from him, she settled the instrument in a safe place at the foot of her blankets, then laid down and pulled the covers up to her chin.

But as she closed her eyes, she couldn't blink away the image of the crimson scar spanning the back of his hand. What manner of adversity had he experienced in this wilderness? She longed to know more.

Tomorrow, she would find out.

CHAPTER 5

*It's not often I'm surprised in this wearisome existence. Maybe because I fear
the lack of control. Yet the irony of that thought mocks me. When have I ever
been truly in control?*
~ Joseph's Journal

*M*onti had to pry her eyelids open the next morning as
the sound of metal clanging forced her awake. She
tried to sit up, blinking against the bright morning light, but every
limb in her body screamed against the movement. Had the single day
on horseback caused this much pain?

She'd thought she was getting tougher after all those weeks on the
train, then in the wagon. If that were the case, though, every inch of
her body wouldn't protest so thoroughly. She clamped her teeth
around her lower lip to hold in a moan.

Joseph knelt beside the fire, his back to her. He must have heard
her movements as she finally reached a sitting position. Or perhaps
the moan stuck in her throat had slipped out.

When he turned to look at her, his eyes seemed brighter than the day before. His face softened and...perhaps that was her imagination but...did the corner of his mouth tip up in the makings of a smile?

She stroked a hand over her hair. What a sight she must look. She'd not bothered to uncoil her chignon before retiring, so her hair must be a mass of loose strands. It was awkward enough sleeping with only this man mere feet away. Back in Montreal, her reputation would be in shreds by now. But out here, there didn't seem to be anyone to see or care.

A frightening thought in itself. She pulled the blankets up around her waist, even though she was fully clothed and wrapped tightly in her coat. At least she had ways to protect herself. Skills she'd worked hard to learn. Although, Joseph didn't seem like the type she'd need to guard against. She could only pray her instincts were true.

"Coffee?"

She glanced back at him.

He held up a tin cup, his brows raised as he awaited her response.

"Oui. Thank you."

He set the cup on the ground, then poured from the pot into the cup. After returning the pot to its original position, he handed the mug to her. She couldn't help but notice how he hadn't used his left hand for any of it. Not fully anyway. He'd rested the base of his palm against the pot as he poured, and once held his arm out for balance. Had he been using only his right hand the day before? She hadn't noticed.

She took the warm metal from him and cupped her hands around the base to savor the heat. "Shall I make breakfast?" She probably shouldn't ask, since she hadn't the first notion what to make or how to prepare it.

She didn't miss the glance he slid her as he returned the pot to its resting spot. "Thought we'd heat up that corn gruel you made last night."

Her stomach threatened to heave up what little it still contained of the stuff. She couldn't bite back the groan this time and pressed a hand to her middle. "Please no. Anything else."

He chuckled. Actually chuckled. Then he stood, raising to his impressive height. "Maybe I'll whip up some corn cakes then."

By the time she'd returned from a short walk into the trees down the creek, he had a shallow pan on the fire and round pancakes sizzling inside it. Her stomach gurgled in hungry appreciation of the aroma wafting up. "What can I do to help?"

"Let me do the cooking." His mouth quirked up on one side as he shot her a glance.

She laughed. This lighter side of Joseph was a pleasant change

He used their lone eating utensil—the large wooden spoon—to flip the cakes over. "Just need to roll up the bedding. After we eat and clean up, we can hit the trail."

She straightened her blankets and rolled them in a tight bundle, then tucked her Bible inside the roll. Next, she packed his blankets. As she worked, a faint scent wafted from the covers—the scent that was his alone. Man and nature in an aroma more pleasing than she would have expected.

The guitar was missing from where she'd placed it the night before. Did he realize she'd helped him to bed? He must.

While she blessed the food and then ate, he loaded the last of their belongings onto the horses, which were already saddled and waiting. It still seemed strange to sit and eat alone, when there were two of them who needed to partake.

Once they were on the trail, the morning passed in relative silence, although the scenery had begun to change. The low rolling hills grew to steeper inclines, still covered in the brown of winter grass. The sun broke through the low clouds, warming the air enough that her breath no longer formed a white cloud.

At one point several hours into the day, she nudged her horse forward, past the two pack horses that trailed Joseph's mount so she was even with him. "Are these as big as the mountains get?"

He gazed around at the terrain. "These are just hills. We'll get to the mountains tomorrow."

She took another look at the landscape growing steeper by the hour. "Have you lived here long?"

"About a year."

She couldn't help a sideways glance at him. He seemed so comfortable here, as if he'd grown up in these hills. "Where did you live before coming to this land?"

"Texas."

Ah. A land she'd heard stories about. Where cattle ran wild and men of every breed escaped to start new lives. So, what other life had Joseph lived in that place?

She didn't quite have the nerve to ask. She'd already pushed into his personal affairs, and his succinct answers seemed to ward her off.

More than anything, she wanted to ask about the scar on his hand. Would that be too personal? Would it anger him?

Joseph stiffened beside her, as though he could read her mind. But a glance at him showed his attention focused in front of them, far into the distance.

Something moved in that direction. A herd of animals? As she studied them, she could see tall figures atop the animals. Men. As they moved closer, they seemed to be clothed in buckskins, so perhaps a group of trappers or freighters.

"Ease back behind me. No sudden movements."

Whoever it was, their presence had Joseph on edge. She obeyed his order, tucking in beside the first pack horse. And when she looked again at the cluster of strangers, she caught sight of long black braids and feathers protruding from their hair.

Indians.

She couldn't seem to take her gaze from the group as they neared, although still at least a hundred yards away. Her horse began to dance beneath her, and she clutched tighter to the saddle and her reins.

"Relax. Your horse can smell your fear. Try not to pull back on the reins." Joseph's soft cadence drifted back to her.

Relax?

They were riding straight into a band of Indians and he wanted her to relax? She exhaled a long breath and forced her arms and legs to loosen. "Are they friendly? What do they want?"

"We'll see shortly."

The Indians were near enough now that they might hear if she spoke again, so she held her tongue. Reaching down, she felt for the garter holding up her stockings. Should she remove the pistol and have it ready? Or wait, relying only on her trust in God and Joseph?

He reached for the rifle in the scabbard attached to his saddle.

A thought slid in that slowed her racing heart. The Lord had sent her out here to minister to a tribe of Indians just like these. In fact, it was possible these were the very Indians who Antoine served. The idea made her sit straighter.

She studied the group again. About a dozen and all men, from what she could tell. They didn't wear paint on their faces like she'd heard stories about. All wore buckskins, and some had furs wrapped around their shoulders.

Joseph reined in his horse when the group was about a dozen strides away, and the Indians did the same. He raised a hand in greeting and spoke a string of words she didn't understand.

The Indian in front nodded and raised his hand in response. Then he answered with another string of words and hand gestures.

Joseph's face grew uncertain, as though he couldn't decipher the rapid fire of language. She didn't blame him. The words seemed to be a mixture of clipped sounds and long vowels. Enchanting, but very foreign. Certainly nothing like the French she'd learned from her earliest days.

Joseph responded to the man with both his hands and voice, but he seemed to stumble through a mixture of English and Indian words.

She nudged her horse forward. If this was the tribe she'd be serving with Antoine, she should introduce herself instead of hanging back like a sullen child. Even if they weren't, it would be best to learn how to interact now.

"How do you say hello in their language?" She murmured her question just loud enough for Joseph to hear.

He jerked his face to her for a split second before turning back to the Indians. In that fraction of time, his look had been a mixture of shock, warning, and...something else. "Kitsiksíksimatsimmo."

It was the whole string of words he'd first said to the Indian. All she wanted was a simple *hello*, but she'd have to trust him on it.

Squaring her shoulders, she turned to the group of natives and offered a pleasant smile. "Kitsiksíksimatsimmo." She'd probably butchered the phrase, but hopefully her intent was clear.

The Indian who seemed to be the leader studied her. His impassive expression looked to be covering a hint of amusement. At least it wasn't anger.

He responded with a slew of sounds in the same cadence as before, then raised his hand to Joseph. He then glanced at Monti once more with that same touch of amusement, raising his hand to her as he turned his horse to the side. The braves behind him followed his direction, and the group moved northward, slightly off from the direction they'd been traveling before.

Joseph nudged his horse, and the other three followed. Monti's pulse raced in her throat, and she took a moment to simply relish the fact that she was alive. She'd just encountered her very first Indians. And spoken to them.

"What did he say?" A giddy feeling bubbled up in her chest as she pushed her horse up beside Joseph's. She'd actually spoken to an Indian, and he'd answered her.

"He said you talk a lot."

A giggle slipped out before she could stop it. "What? No, he didn't. What did he really say?"

Joseph slid her a sideways glance. "Close to that. I'm not real good with the language yet, but it was something about courage and speaking." He shrugged. "That translates to talks-a-lot in my book. I tend to agree with him."

She let out a huff. "If you think I speak overmuch, you should have heard my mother."

The silence settled back over them, which was fine, because it gave her mind time to replay the scene with the Indians and remember how each had looked.

"Did your mother speak English or French?" Joseph's question pulled her attention in a wholly different direction.

"Both. English was her first language, but she learned French when she met my papa."

"Did she remarry? I mean...after your father..." He seemed to struggle with the best way to word his question, and she rushed into her answer to save him.

"No. Mama was good with business and kept food on our table by selling Papa's inventions. She loved business and could sell anything to anyone. She was a remarkable woman."

"Inventions?" The curiosity in his tone was the first unveiled interest she'd heard from him.

"My papa was an engineer. A genius, they say. He invented several things, but the most famous was a kind of electromagnetic relay that could be used for sending messages along a wire."

"Really? The wire carried notes?"

She shook her head. Mama was much better at providing an understandable explanation, but she'd heard it enough to give the basics. "Pulses could be recognized through the wire. The sender and receiver only needed to work out a code between them, and they could communicate effectively. Lots of businesses found it useful for communicating from one building to another. She sold the system all over Europe through her agents there." It was a wonder what Mama had accomplished. "People said my father was a genius, but I think Mama might have been the smarter of the two."

He didn't respond, just rode on quietly. Perhaps she'd talked overlong on the subject, but the memories of her parents were all she had left. She held on to those memories, especially those of Mama.

~

The more Joseph learned about her, the more of an enigma she became. This little French princess had obviously been raised in a comfortable life. Yet she seemed to possess more nerve and tenacity than he'd given her credit for.

Her mother must have been tough to continue her husband's business after his death. And Miss Bergeron had obviously learned some of that same skill. She'd faced the Indians without quaking in her boots and with an equal measure of kindness and spunk.

That was good, because she'd be faced with plenty more opportunities that would test her mettle the longer she stayed in this wild land.

They were moving closer to the mountain country now, and patches of snow littered the grass, especially where clusters of trees gathered. The temperature seemed to be sinking, and the low, gray clouds signaled snow coming soon. Probably tonight. Which meant they should camp early enough to prepare for it.

A patch of snow ahead caught his notice. The barren spot in the center of it seemed an odd color. Not the tan of winter grass or the brown of mud. This spot was crimson. Must be a recent animal kill. Perhaps from that wolf pack they'd heard the night before.

He slid a glance at Miss Bergeron. She was stroking her mare's mane as she rode, apparently not seeing the remains of the slaughter.

Should he steer them away so she didn't notice the gory sight? If she were going to remain in this land, she'd need to resign herself to not only see it, but be willing to prepare meals from the flesh of animals. Of course, perhaps they should start with a lesson on how not to burn the food first.

Keeping them on the same trajectory they'd been traveling, he didn't comment about the patch of blood, fur, and bones until Miss Bergeron sucked in a breath.

She pointed to the spot. "What happened there?"

"Looks like an animal kill." He tried to keep his voice casual, letting her know this was nothing out of the ordinary.

"Do you think it's from the wolves we heard last night?" So she'd put the pieces together too. Good.

"Hard to know. I hope that's the case. If their bellies are full, they won't search out more prey for a while."

She nodded, but another glance at her revealed faint indentations above her brows, as though she were thinking hard, or maybe troubled about something. At least she didn't squeal or act squeamish.

Yet, even though she could ride by a bloody carcass without swooning, how would she manage the rest of the savage wildness of this land?

CHAPTER 6

Lord, make me attentive to the needs of those around me. Let me hear their
silent longings and be the instrument of Your blessing.
~ Monti's Journal

*M*onti took in steady breaths of the cool—nay, icy—air. Her exhale swirled around her face as she burrowed into her coat. "I'm going to need warmer clothing than I anticipated. It didn't get this cold in Montreal." The sun had dipped past the far tree line, causing all warmth to evaporate as if it feared the coming darkness.

"I bought you fabric at the fort." Joseph's warm voice rumbled beside her. "Figured you might need something warmer. Brown was the only color they had, but it's wool, so it'll be better than that flimsy stuff you're wearing. Buckskin would be best, but it'll take a while to tan hides for a set of clothes."

She looked at him, letting a smile slip onto her face. "Monsieur Malcom. I do believe that's the most you've spoken to me yet."

His neck and cheeks darkened a bit. "Just thought I'd let you know."

She nodded. *"Merci beaucoup.* I appreciate it." This man was full of all manner of surprises.

He motioned toward a small cluster of trees. "We'll stop there. It'll probably snow tonight, so we'd best set up a cover."

Brrr. Just the thought of sleeping out in the open air while snow fluttered down around them sounded frightfully cold. She pulled the coat tighter around her neck. "Just tell me how I can help."

She'd watched Joseph all day and hadn't noticed anything unusual about the way he did or didn't use his left hand, but riding a steady saddle horse didn't offer many situations where he would be required to use that particular appendage.

But as she assisted with small tasks to help set up the oilcloth covering over their campsite, it became clear he went to great lengths not to use the muscles in his left hand. Not that he was obvious about it. He compensated well with the wrist and palm on that side. But every so often she would see a flicker of frustration cross his face. Not pain, just an obvious irritation with himself.

She was dying to ask what had happened, but she'd seen men become angry when faced with their limitations. She'd have to wait for the right opening.

After he unloaded the packs from the horses and started pulling supplies from their wrappings, she approached. "Can I help prepare the evening meal?"

He looked up at her. Really looked, not the sideways glances he'd been sending all day, as though he was trying to pretend he didn't care about her existence. This was a full-on scrutiny, like he was weighing whether he should trust her with the task again.

She forced herself to hold his gaze, no squirming. "I've not cooked much before, but I'm a fast learner. If you show me how, I won't let it burn again." She hated to feel like she was begging, but this was a skill she needed to learn. And he'd already done so much for her—coming to fetch her and handling almost all the chores himself—the least she could do would be to take on this one task for herself.

"I thought we'd put on a pot of beans for tonight and the morning. If you're extra hungry, we can fry corncakes to hold us over while the beans cook."

That sounded heavenly. The meager leftover corncake and dried meat they'd eaten midday had left her hours ago.

She knelt beside the pack of cornmeal and pulled the pot from the stack of supplies Joseph had piled. "What else goes in the corncakes, and how much of each?"

Lord willing, she'd get it right this time.

~

The snow began just as darkness settled securely over the land. Monti sat before the fire, tucking the fur tighter around her as she stared up at the silvery flakes floating down. The ones over the fire disappeared when they neared the flames.

Joseph sat on his pallet, staring out into the same white-specked darkness. Their blankets were positioned a bit closer this time, out of necessity. There was only so much oilcloth to stretch above them, and not even *she* would force him to sleep in the falling snow just to ensure the fire separated them. As it was, the bedrolls formed the shape of an L.

"I guess this isn't the first snowfall of the year, since we've seen bits along the trail. Does the snow ever completely melt through the winter months?"

He glanced at her. "Didn't last winter." Something dark tinged his voice. "The ice stayed all the way through May. And in the mountains, some of it never melted."

She studied him. Why did he speak of the winter as if he hated it? "You don't like snow?"

He stared off into the distance again. "Snow and ice are a fact of this land. You have to make peace with them, or winter will eat you alive."

Such ominous words. Maybe ice had contributed to his injury. But the hard look in his expression kept her from asking.

Perhaps a change of topic would help. "Do you have any family in the area?"

His face softened a fraction. "A sister and her husband." The corners of his mouth tipped. "A niece who's just learning to walk. My aunt and uncle live across the valley from them."

She took a moment to picture the scene he'd described. "I can't even imagine having that much family. Much less all in one place. Do they live near you?"

He sent her a sardonic look. "I suppose. Sometimes. There's a cave I use a few hours up the mountain."

"You don't have a home?" She shouldn't let her tone sound so incredulous, but...he had nothing?

His shoulders lifted in a casual shrug. "I don't need one. I keep a few supplies in the cave. Emma insists I stay with them when I come to visit. But mostly, I prefer to sleep on the trail."

She took in this new bit of information, working to transform her image of him. She'd imagined at least a quaint cabin somewhere. Maybe nestled at the base of a mountain, beside a stream where he caught fish and beaver.

He was truly a nomad, though. No wonder he seemed so deeply entrenched in this land, even though he'd been here less than a twelve-month. Would she be the same after her first year? With God's strength, she hoped she would feel a little more equipped for the work ahead than she did now. His work.

After several more moments of quiet, both of them studying the falling snow, an idea struck her. She turned to Joseph. "Would you mind if I play the guitar you brought along? I've played the violin for years, but haven't ever tried a larger instrument. I'd like to see how different it is."

His brows came low, as if the idea angered him. But then he seemed to reconsider his reaction, and his expression turned blank. "That instrument belongs to my sister's husband. It's a Christmas present, and she asked me to bring it back for her."

A stab of disappointment filtered through her. The guitar had seemed like something special to him last night. Like something that might help him open up some. But if it was a gift for his relative, she couldn't press him to bring it out.

She nodded, trying not to show her disappointment. "I see."

The silence threatened to settle over them until Joseph pushed to his feet. "I suppose 'tis not a problem if we're careful."

He disappeared into the darkness, then returned a moment later with the guitar. The firelight danced on the sleekness of the dark wood as he crossed to her and nestled the instrument in her lap.

She settled it, the bulk of the base so much larger than she was accustomed to. She had to work to lean over far enough to see the strings. Her hands found the chords easily, especially since the guitar had frets to guide her. Much easier than her violin, where precision was so important.

She tried a simple strum. A nice sound, but nothing so difficult as a song. The sonatas she'd memorized wouldn't work on this instrument, and her mind went blank as she struggled to summon other music she might be able to adapt.

A glance at Joseph showed he was sitting on his bedroll again, watching her. Perhaps... "Could you teach me a song? I can't think of any music in my violin repertoire that could be played on this."

His gaze turned wary. "I can't play it."

She tilted her head at him. Was he just saying that so he wouldn't have to teach her? She'd heard him last night, and the easy way he'd carried it to her showed he was quite familiar with holding such an instrument. Not to mention the hint of longing that had shadowed his eyes as he'd handed it to her.

What song might they both have heard? She raised her brows at him. "Do you know 'The Green Willow Tree?'" It was a fun old ballad. A bit jaunty, and would certainly liven up the evening.

His brow lowered. "Maybe."

"Can you teach me? I know the tune and words, but not the chording nor how to strum."

He studied her for a long moment. Or perhaps he was thinking through the song. His face held such a contrast of expressions it was hard to tell. Then at last, "The chords are simple." He gave her the progression, which was, indeed, simple.

She formed each chord with a strum, then added the words their cook used to sing as she baked pies. For some reason, this long-winded ballad had been the woman's favorite pie-baking accompaniment.

"There was a ship that sailed on the Northern Sea.

She went by the name of the Green Willow Tree.

I'm afraid she'll be taken by the enemy,

For she sails on the lowlands low."

She paused after that first verse to see Joseph's response. The faint glimmer of a smile touched his eyes, giving her the hope to push a little further. "What rhythm should I be strumming with my right hand?"

He squinted, his hand tapping his leg as he must be replaying the verse in his mind. "A simple, dat, dat-da-dat, dat, dat, for each line." He tapped his leg with his right hand as he spoke the rhythm.

She tried it, stroking down with each "dat." It sounded clumsy and rushed, certainly not right.

"No, it goes down, down-up-down, up, down." He spoke the words with the same tapping rhythm.

She tried again, but this time her strumming seemed to have no rhythm at all. Blowing out a breath, she pursed her lips. "It'd be so much easier if I could just glide a bow across the strings."

He chuckled, then shifted. Before she realized what he was doing, he stood and came to crouch in front of her. He slipped the glove off his right hand, revealing the strong, muscled grip of a man accustomed to working hard in the elements.

Resting his left hand—still gloved—on top of the guitar, he positioned his right hand over the strings near the round opening in the body. He didn't meet her eyes, but nodded toward her hand on the frets. "Start from the beginning."

He was so close, even though almost a foot separated their shoulders. She could feel his strength with every fiber of her being.

Swallowing the lump in her throat, she forced herself to ignore his overwhelming presence and focus on the chords. When her hand was positioned, he tapped out the rhythm once, then strummed it.

She was a bit slow on the first chord change, but settled into the flow easily as he strummed a lively tune. After a couple lines, she started singing the first verse again.

As she moved into the second, she could hear the rich vibrato of him humming, and it swelled an ache in her chest, not unlike what she'd experienced in the midst of an emotional sonata. Music always had a powerful effect over her, but playing with this man moved it to a deeper level.

As the third verse moved into the chorus line, his humming turned into singing. Harmony that perfectly accented her melody. He sang in a low tenor. A deliciously rich sound.

As they entered the tenth short verse, where the words told the story of the ship's cabin boy drilling holes in the underbelly of an attacking enemy ship, she slid a glance at Joseph.

He met her smile with a happy glimmer in his gaze, not breaking the rhythm of his singing or playing.

After the last line of the closing verse, they ran through the chord progression a final time, Joseph ending with a rapid strum for the finale.

She couldn't help the thrill pulsing through her as she turned a grin on him. "That was perfect. The best rendition I've ever heard."

His mouth tipped in an off-kilter grin. "I suppose it wasn't half bad."

The power of that grin set off a flurry in her chest. Enough to make her yearn for much more.

CHAPTER 7

Just when I thought the penalty for my sins had been paid...
~ Joseph's Journal

When Joseph awoke the next morning, a clean white blanket had settled over the land. He'd slept like a man with a clear conscience, although that description hardly applied to him. Still, after the soul-stirring music he and Monti had played, his muscles had relaxed more than any time he could remember since the accident.

His nerves, however... Sitting so close to Miss Bergeron had brought every one of them to awareness, his blood coursing through his body in a way that proved he was still very much alive.

A glance at the woman showed she still slept, cocooned under her blankets and furs so that only the top of her head and her eyes peeked out from the coverings.

The sun was just rising over the tree line, which meant they were later getting started than the day before. But she looked so peaceful. His gaze swept back to her, and he let his eyes linger. Those pert brows, her perfectly shaped, expressive eyes. Even the shape of her forehead looked elegant. Regal.

She was so intensely beautiful, it was almost painful to look at her. Especially knowing he was taking her into a land so harsh and unforgiving. The wilderness cared not how exquisite she was. She would be put through the same rigors as every other person, maybe even more. How would she emerge after the testing? Would she let it beat her down? From what he'd seen so far, he had a feeling she'd give even the harshest mountain winter a valiant battle.

Or maybe...perhaps she would charm this land into compliance, the way she'd coaxed him into playing the guitar last night.

He turned away. He was probably letting himself get too close to her. Once he deposited her at Father Bergeron's cabin, he'd likely not see her more than once a year. If she survived.

He was just coaxing the embers of their fire back to life when he heard a tiny mewing sound behind him. He made the mistake of turning to look.

She was stretching, but stopped when he turned, then gave him a sheepish little smile that sent his pulse bolting through his chest.

"Good morning." Her voice had that sweet, sluggish quality brought on by sleep, and his body reacted by clogging his own throat so he couldn't respond.

He nodded in answer, then turned back to the fire. He cleared his throat and finally found words. "It'll be a minute before I have coffee ready, so you might as well stay where it's warm." The thought was all too alluring, so he jumped to his feet and grabbed the kettle. "I'm going to get water."

Maybe a dip in the icy creek would douse the ruckus inside his body.

"o you still think we'll arrive at my cousin's home by evening?" Monti ducked against an icy breeze that tried to slide between her coat and neck. It'd been hours since they'd stopped for the midday meal, but the dense gray clouds hanging low offered no sign of how late it might be.

"Probably not today. The weather's slowing us down a bit." Joseph rode beside her, not hunched as she was, but sitting tall and straight in the saddle.

Not today. That meant another frigid night. Possibly a fourth day fighting this wind and blowing snow. They'd been climbing hills and skirting mountains all morning, but at least the snow had stopped. This flurry of white was only the wind whipping the stuff off the ground.

"We'll need to ride single file through this gap." He motioned toward an opening between a rocky cliff on one side and a huge boulder on the other. "Stay behind the pack horses, but close."

She nodded, then reined her mare in to let the other horses pass. She'd become amazingly comfortable handling the horse after more than two days of solid riding. Of course, Velvet was a sweet mare. Willing to do whatever she asked.

As Joseph entered the narrow opening between the rocks, an urgency slid through her chest. "Be careful." Although he was the last person she should worry about being in danger. Joseph knew his way in this place like a fish in a lake.

His shoulders tensed—enough to make the action clear even across the distance that separated them—and perhaps that was why a knot of fear balled in her middle.

Father, protect us. Please. She nudged her horse closer to the second pack horse trailing behind Joseph's mount. The loaded animal surged forward, crowding the horse in front of it.

It all seemed to happen at once. One of the horses bucked, a tail flying up in the air. The horse behind it jerked backward, slamming into the cliff on their left.

An animal squealed. Screamed.

A terrific crack sounded overhead.

"Yah!" Joseph yelled. The horses in front of her jerked forward.

Monti's own mare bolted with them as though she were dragged by a tether line. Monti grabbed at the saddle, scrambling to catch hold before she slid off the back.

Another sound from above, a screeching, sliding noise.

Before she could secure herself in the saddle, icy cold snow streamed over her. She didn't have time to process what was happening before the horse jerked sideways.

The force of the cold slammed into her. She was tumbling. Her foot snagged on the saddle, then loosened as she lost all contact with the horse.

Frigid, icy softness swallowed her. Covering her completely. Wrapping her in darkness. Silence. Were her eyes closed? No, the mass of ice seemed to be pressing on her everywhere.

Someone yelled—Joseph—from a long way away. She fought to find him. To claw out of this silent tomb that pressed down on her.

She created a little pocket of air around her face, then kicked to free her legs, but she couldn't move them more than an inch or two. She worked to right herself, but too much snow covered her.

A muffled noise sounded, like a scraping in the ice above her.

Joseph.

She pawed at the snow closest to the sound for minutes that seemed to take hours. Cold and wet seeped under her sleeves, inside her gloves.

Then her hand struck something hard. She scrambled for it. Grappling as her fingers fought through the snow.

And then, though she still couldn't see more than the dim white around her face, her hand broke through the surface. Another hand grasped hers.

Joseph.

She clung to him with all the strength left in her. He held tight, a grip so strong it hurt. Yet, she wouldn't trade the pain for anything.

Except maybe a good strong breath.

The air inside her little hole didn't seem as satisfying as it had at first. Maybe her lungs were just struggling under the pressure of the snow.

Joseph's hand loosened around hers, then slid away. She scrambled for him again, but then cool air filtered in through the hole his hand vacated. She inhaled deeply. His voice came, sounding as though it were far away. "Hold this arm for a minute. I need that hand to dig you out."

The stiffness of his buckskin coat touched her hand, and she gripped it. After groping for a moment, she wrapped her fingers around his wrist.

She could feel the ice around her shifting, hear the scratching, see the snow above her glowing brighter as daylight filtered through it.

Then at last. Light so blinding she had to close her eyes. She pawed at the snow, helping him clear it off her.

Then he pulled her up to a sitting position, one hand on her upper arm and the other behind her back.

"Oh..." She tried to form coherent words, but her teeth began chattering the moment she opened her mouth.

"Let's get you out." He shifted to work on the snow still bogging down her legs and skirts.

At last, she could move her legs, and she pulled them up under her so she could stand. He helped her rise, steadying her when her legs threatened to buckle.

She took a step forward, but the snow seemed to give way beneath her. Then Joseph was there in front of her, catching her with the breadth of his chest.

She clutched at him, grabbing fists full of his buckskin coat. His hands came around her waist, holding her tight. Secure. She sank deeper into that hold, burying her face in the safety of his strength. Her chattering teeth quieted as his warmth seeped around her.

"Monti." He seemed to breathe her in with the word. And she could feel the scruff of his cheek against the top of her head, the warmth of his breath there.

She pressed in further. This man would take care of her no matter what besieged them. Every part of her knew it to be true.

After a long moment, she inhaled a deep breath and released it in a shaky stream. Then she straightened, letting the cold air come between them. Looking up into his face, she took in the earnest way he studied her. The tinge of fear coloring his eyes a deep brown.

She tried to summon a smile. "Thank you for saving me."

He nodded, his throat working. "Are you all right? Hurt anywhere?"

She ran a quick check on her extremities. Her toes had gone mostly numb, but that had taken place long before the dump of snow buried her. "I'm fine. Truly."

Turning to look back at the pile of white, then up at the top of the cliff, she had to shield her eyes from the glare of sun. "What happened?"

"When the horse bumped the rock, it must have loosened a snowdrift up there. It's a miracle you weren't hurt worse."

She turned to look at him, then. A miracle? The snow had buried her several feet under, but with Joseph here, he'd been able to pull her out right away. His words seemed a bit extreme. But maybe he'd experienced something similar in his past, and it'd turned out much worse for him. She couldn't help a glance at his left hand, but she forced her gaze not to linger there. "I'm thankful God brought you here to protect me."

He blew out a frosty breath and looked away from her, then turned back and held out his right hand. "Do you think you can ride a few more minutes? As soon as we reach trees where we'll be protected from the elements, we can stop for the night. Build a fire and let you dry out."

"I can go on." Her legs were icy from the dampness that had soaked through her stockings, but she would last as long as she had to. Placing her gloved hand in his, she shifted her skirts and wobbled through the deep snow.

Her horse was standing with his, and he helped her back in the saddle. They were on their way soon enough, but she couldn't help replaying the events in her mind. The fear that engulfed her as she was buried in the darkness. The way he'd used his left hand as more of a broom than a shovel, never moving the fingers. The way he'd clung to her, wrapping her in his strength.

That feeling alone was enough to warm her all the way to her core, despite the icy winds swirling around them.

～

*T*hat evening, Joseph had to push himself through the steps to set-up camp and settle the horses. His mind kept replaying the moment he realized Monti had been buried in the snow. The terror surging through his chest. His inability to dig through the icy mass quickly enough with his one working hand.

And then...that moment when he'd clutched her tight against himself. She'd fit so perfectly, wrapped in his arms. He'd felt—just for a moment—as though he had something to offer her. Maybe it was just the rush of relief that she'd not died under the avalanche. The fact that he'd been there to dig her out. But she made him feel...more alive than he had any time since the accident. Better, too.

She followed him around more this evening than she had before, helping as she could. Perhaps she sensed the fear that prickled just under his surface. The fear of letting her get too far away. Outside of the reach of his protection. They were safer together than apart in this unrelenting country.

"The horses have all eaten. I can prepare our meal now." Monti moved toward him and knelt to place the pot beside the fire he was nurturing.

"This will take a few more minutes before it's hot enough for cooking." He sat back on his heels as the fire finally caught hold of the dry saplings he'd found for kindling. The flame ate away at the wood, almost ready for more substantial fare.

"Did you have something in mind for the meal tonight? Or I can make corncakes again. I'm doing better with not burning them."

He glanced at her, taking in the hesitant look so different than the confidence she'd started the trip with. In truth, she'd come far since that first day when she'd been as prickly as a Texas cactus. "Anything you make would be much appreciated."

Her eyes seemed to light at his comment, and she straightened. "I'll get water."

While she worked with the foodstuffs, he checked the horses a final time. The weary animals had already begun to doze on the picket line, so he left them to rest and returned to the fire. Monti was packing the cornmeal mixture into small cakes. "I can't seem to get these to stick together like you did."

He could help her, but she was doing well enough, and she made such a fetching sight working there over the pan. So, he wrapped his arms around his legs and stayed put. "Add a little more water. Eggs are the best to hold it all together, but we don't have any. My sister uses eggs and a dash of milk, and all kinds of herbs to season hers. Of course, she happens to have all those things handy in her well-stocked larder."

Monti glanced over at him, curiosity lighting her eyes. "Your sister who lives near your aunt and uncle? The one with the little girl?"

He nodded. "They're my only family left. And Emma's my twin, so it's nice to have her close." Why had he said that? Maybe because he hoped it would bring on the look that now softened Monti's features.

"Your twin sister? How special. I hope I get to meet her one day. Are they near my cousin's mission?"

He raised his brows at the formal way she referred to Father Bergeron's simple cabin. "A couple hours' ride. I'm sure Em would love to meet you. I think she misses having a woman nearer her age to talk to. And Hannah will love you."

Her delicate mouth formed an angelic smile. "Hannah is your niece?"

He nodded, not quite able to shift his eyes away from those dainty lips. That smile. "She's cute as a baby bunny. Has the same color eyes as me and Em, and little brown curls."

She was looking in his eyes now that he'd called attention to them. He shouldn't have mentioned them, but the way she held his gaze made him not regret the attention quite as much. This woman had a way of making him feel like he wasn't quite as deficient as he knew himself to be. If only he could be the man he saw reflected in her eyes just now.

He broke the contact and turned away, rubbing his gloved hands on his legs.

"You said before you lived in Texas. Were you a frontiersman there too? I've never been to the United States, although I hear parts of Texas are as unsettled as this land."

He slid a quick glance at her. Did he dare share the details of that former life? What would she think of him then? Before he could think through the matter, he let his answer slip out. "I was a law clerk in Texas."

She stared at him, that delicate mouth forming a perfect O.

He looked away again. She could think what she'd like.

"Do you jest?" That French lilt came back into her tone, drawing him. He forced himself to resist its pull to study her.

"I jest not. It was the most boring time of my life." He reached for a log and positioned it on the fire. "When Emma needed someone to take her north, I jumped at the chance. That's one decision I'll never regret."

~

*M*onti replayed his words in her mind. *That's one decision I'll never regret.* As if he lived with the pain of other choices he would change if he could.

Such an enigma this man was. She'd known he wasn't simply an uneducated boor. He spoke too well for that to be the case. When he spoke at all, that was. But a law clerk? She studied him, trying to picture wire-rimmed spectacles framing those clear amber eyes. Bent over a desk with pen held tightly in ink-stained fingers.

The sight seemed so at odds with the rugged man sitting across from her, a giggle bubbled up her throat. She caught it just as the sound escaped her mouth in a sort of chortle. Pressing a hand to her neck, she smiled at him. "I must say, that wasn't quite what I expected. I suppose the mountain wilderness doesn't offer much work for a law clerk. Is that what made you change professions?"

He shrugged. "My father was the one who secured that job for me.

He was an attorney. I never much liked being shut indoors all the time, even though it was sometimes a welcome reprieve from the scorching sun. A Texas summer could be as hot as the winter up here is cold."

She scrambled for another question, anything to keep him talking. He'd never been this free with words, especially about himself. "And what of the town where you grew up? You said that was Baltimore?"

Reaching forward with his right hand, he tossed another log on the fire but kept hold of a strip of the wooden fiber. This he twisted around his finger as he spoke. "Baltimore was hot, too. A muggy kind of heat, but not as bad as Texas."

What else could she ask that wouldn't sound like prying? So many of the questions that sprang to mind were rather personal, but she chose one and hoped for the best. "Where did you learn to play the guitar?"

He didn't answer right away. She watched him from the corner of her gaze. A direct stare probably would have spooked him, but if she needed to retract her question, she'd only know it by watching his expression.

He seemed to be remembering, his gaze locked on the fire as his fingers twisted that sliver of wood. "Our neighbor in Baltimore taught me. He was an Irishman, so I learned a lot of old Irish folk songs. I practiced when I could and learned how to pick out tunes to the other songs I knew."

As she'd suspected. His easy manner of handling the guitar made it clear the instrument had been a long-time friend. A lifetime companion, it sounded like.

Everything within her wanted to ask about his injury. Would he ever be able to play an instrument with that hand? Yet something held her back. Maybe it was the fact that he'd finally opened up and revealed a little of himself.

The last thing she wanted was to put that dark look back on his face.

CHAPTER 8

When I should be most unnerved, my Father places gifts along the way.
Tokens of His love for me.
~ Monti's Journal

*A*ntoine had aged.

It was Monti's first thought as her father's cousin descended from the cabin's doorway to meet them in the snow. She stepped into his warm embrace, the one she'd loved as a girl whenever he came to visit them in Montreal. She always imagined hugs from her father would have felt like this. Maybe they had, and she'd replaced those early memories of Papa with Antoine's visits.

"I have missed you." She could barely push the words through the lump in her throat, and he responded with another squeeze.

Then he pulled back, gripping her elbows as he studied her face. "How are you, *ma fifille?*"

Monti smiled through her blurry vision at the old nickname. *My little girl.* She'd forgotten how much that simple moniker warmed her all the way through. "I am well. Very well now that we've finally reached you. And what of you? How do you fare?"

He patted her arm, then released her. "Blessed. God is bringing forth fruit from our efforts, and it gives me much joy." He motioned past her. "Monsieur Malcom. You have accomplished your task with excellence. I cannot thank you enough for bringing my girl to me."

She turned to catch Joseph's reaction. From the first moment they met, she'd not been what he expected, which she knew had made his job much harder than he'd planned. Yet, once he'd pushed past his initial shock, he'd been kind and respectful, if a bit reserved. So unlike the type of men she'd learned to guard against.

He nodded toward Antoine as he held both their reins in his hand. "Glad to help."

She couldn't keep herself from adding on to that understated comment. "Joseph has been a gift from God, bringing me safely through the wilderness. He even saved me from an avalanche."

The lines etched in Antoine's forehead creased deeper. "Praise be to God for His protection."

Joseph cleared his throat, scuffing his foot in the packed snow. "I'll settle Miss Bergeron's horse in the lean-to, then be on my way. Good to see you, Father."

Monti straightened, a bit of uneasiness stirring in her chest. "You can't leave yet. Stay and have the midday meal with us." She glanced at her cousin. She'd not even stepped foot in his home, and already she was inviting people to eat at his table. But surely he wouldn't mind.

"Of course. You must stay and break bread with us." Antoine stepped forward. "I will settle the horses. You both go in and warm yourselves."

Her cousin took one of the horses' reins from Joseph, though he seemed reluctant to give them up. Monti couldn't help the smile that tightened her chest as the two traipsed around the side of the cabin.

At the last moment, Antoine turned toward her. "Go in and settle your things, *ma chère*."

She nodded, and as they disappeared past the corner of the building, she turned to see her new home.

She'd tried not to create any preconceptions about what Antoine's home would look like. It was the base for his missionary work, after all. But somehow, she'd not expected a rough-hewn log cabin. Not as barren and dark as this structure. The walls seemed sturdy enough, however the door looked to be only two hand-cut boards held together by a couple of crossbeams. The cracks between the boards hadn't been chinked as the walls were, so the wind could easily blow through. In fact, those cracks were wide enough for a person to peer inside.

As the door bounced shut behind her, darkness seemed to settle over the place. A fire in the hearth on the far left provided most of the light for the room. In the center, a trestle table held a lantern and a book—maybe a Bible—as well as several papers and an ink pot and quill. Benches lined the table, and a bedtick on the floor in the corner seemed to be the only other pieces of furniture. Crates sat stacked against the far right wall.

She'd promised a meal to Joseph, so she stepped toward the hearth first. The pot hanging there might hold food, if she were lucky. Inside, the bubbling, lumpy mass seemed to be stew. Just enough for the three of them, hopefully. She found a few dishes stacked on a small shelf beside the fireplace.

By the time Antoine stepped into the cabin with Joseph close on his heels, she had two finely carved bowls set out on the table, filled with stew. Since she'd only found the two bowls, she opted to use a tin cup for her own meal. And she'd filled the remaining cups with what seemed to be tea in the kettle.

"Place those packs here, beside the crates." Antoine motioned toward the floor on the far end of the cabin.

Joseph seemed to have off-loaded most of the bundles from one of the pack horses, and now eased them down where the priest pointed.

"Our Peigan friends will appreciate these gifts." Antoine sent a smile to Joseph that seemed almost fatherly. Then he swept his gaze over the table, landing on her. "You have been busy. I hope you found everything you sought. My humble home will blossom under your care, I can see."

She could feel the surge of heat rise to her cheeks, but she motioned to the benches. "I've only served the food that was already prepared. We should eat before it cools."

She'd placed her setting beside what she had assumed would be Antoine's seat, but her cousin took the opposite side. Joseph allowed her to settle on the bench first, touching her elbow to balance her when she wobbled as she lifted her leg over. His touch sent a warmth all the way up her arm, but she did her best to ignore it.

When they were seated, Antoine bowed his head and spoke a simple prayer of gratefulness. Her heart swelled as she raised her own thanks to the Father. For bringing her here safely. For sending Joseph to accompany her. For placing this gentle man of God in her family and providing this place of refuge after her world in Montreal collapsed.

Just before Antoine spoke the amen, she glanced sideways at Joseph. His head was bowed, but his eyes stayed open, staring down at the table. Glassy. Something about his expression seemed void. As though he'd retreated to a distant place.

She didn't have time to dwell on it though, because Antoine began peppering them with questions as soon as they started into their stew.

After he'd extracted the exciting elements about their journey from Joseph, he turned his focus on her. "And tell me, my cousin. Were you able to settle your mama's business affairs suitably? I am sorry I could not come to you myself."

The all too familiar wad of emotion surged in her throat, but she nodded. "Oui. Our steward agreed to take over the business. He paid for the rights to Papa's inventions, and I signed it all to him." Done. Perhaps she should have stayed and continued the work Papa and Mama had both taken such pride in, but matters of business held no allure for her. The chance to start over, to build a new life in this place of beginnings—the idea had called to her for some time now. If she could make a difference for at least one person, share the faith that had grounded her throughout her years, but especially these past few months, she would call herself blessed.

After they finished the meager meal, Joseph pushed to his feet. He seemed to be scanning the room, taking in the simplicity of it. "I brought in a stack of furs you can use for an extra pallet. Would you like me to string up some ropes before I go? You can use blankets to section off part of the room."

Her gaze swept to the little cot in the corner. Antoine would find it hard to spend the nights on the floor, with the aches and pains increased years sometimes brought. She'd happily continue sleeping on the furs she'd been using. It was a wonder how comfortable and warm they could be. But a little privacy would be more than appreciated.

"Yes, that is good." Her cousin was already motioning toward the cot. "I have rope. We can hang it over here."

She didn't argue the point yet. It would be easier to convince him when it was just the two of them. Then they could move the cot to the opposite corner, and she'd position the furs in the partitioned area.

With Joseph's height and strength, they had the blankets hung in short order. He tied the knots with only the wrist of his left hand and the fingers of his right, and even managed to make the effort look natural.

She still hadn't found the courage to ask about his injury. Would she never learn of it?

As Joseph finally bid them good-night and rode off into the dusky light of late afternoon, she couldn't help the tightening in her chest. Lord willing, Joseph Malcom wouldn't fade from her life just yet. There was still so much she wanted to know about him.

~

"*How* far away do the Indians live?" Monti took another sip of her tea the next morning as she studied Antoine.

He spooned a bite of porridge into his mouth. "Less than an hour's ride." He seemed to be moving laboriously this morning, despite the fact that he'd said he wanted to get an early start.

If she knew what else to do to ready them, she would be up and about the work. But her cousin had said to sit and prepare herself, so she was doing exactly that. Asking all the questions that had lingered in her mind for weeks.

"What do the women spend their days doing?"

Antoine raised his gaze to her, a hint of a sparkle in one of his eyes. "Cooking, caring for the children. The things any wife busies herself with. Would you please bring my Bible here?"

She straightened and rose to obey his request. He must read Scripture just before departing for his work. That would make sense.

After placing the book in front of his bowl, she took her seat again.

"Now, read at the first letter to the Thessalonians. That is where I last stopped."

She slid the book to rest in front of her, found the spot, and started in, trying her best to still her restless mind and focus on the words. The doing would happen soon. For now, she needed to prepare her heart and mind.

She'd barely started into the second verse when the sound of a horse drifted in through the front door. She jerked her head up. "Someone is here." She'd been under the impression Antoine lived a distance away from any neighbors. Had someone heard of her coming and made the trip to welcome her?

He nodded, as though he wasn't surprised by the news. "Welcome him in."

Him. Antoine must be expecting someone he hadn't told her about.

She rose and went to the door. After removing the brace that held it shut, she pulled the door open enough to peer outside.

Joseph Malcom met her gaze, his boot poised on the stoop as if he'd been about to climb up and knock.

She pulled the door open all the way and smiled through the rush of relief. "Good morning. I didn't except to see you again so soon."

He touched two fingers to the fur hood of his coat, as though tapping a hat brim. "Mornin'. I told the Father I'd help tote those supplies to the Indian town. It's too much to carry behind your saddles."

She couldn't stop the flush that crept up her neck, although why it came on, she couldn't have said. Instead she turned away. "Come in and have a cup of tea."

As she filled a mug, she attempted to analyze why his coming made the day seem less daunting. The supplies would have been a challenge for them to transport, so an extra set of hands would be welcome. And perhaps he could help translate if the Indians didn't know English. When her mind brought up the idea that having Joseph Malcom by her side would make any challenge less frightening, she pushed the thought down.

The Lord had made her a capable woman. Fully able to accomplish whatever He set before her. She didn't have to have this man at her side to carry out her mission.

～

*W*ithin a half hour, Joseph had the supplies loaded on his pack horse, and he and the priest saddled the other two mounts.

Monti looked fresh as a rose—a delicate French rose—as she came out in her fur coat with a flowered gown peeking out the bottom. "I've packed some food we can eat today. I hope this will be enough."

He took the bundle from her and tied it behind her saddle. "The Indians might offer food at midday, but this'll be good to have in case." She appeared to be doing her best to handle her part, no matter how limited her experience seemed to be. Maybe he could teach her how to cook a few more dishes. Or Emma could. She was a much better cook than he was.

But then again, maybe he should just step out of Monti's life and let her do what she'd come out here to do. Father Bergeron could teach her all she needed to know, including the cooking.

But the French priest might not be able to keep her safe from the danger that constantly threatened out here. Joseph fought the clenching of his gut with that thought. He used his teeth to jerk the knot tight around the bundle. That danger was exactly why he'd offered to come today. There was no telling how the Indians would accept her. Or whether some cocky young brave would take too much of a fancy to her, beautiful as she was.

She needed more protection than the kind old priest could offer.

Thankfully, Father Bergeron kept Monti occupied as they rode to the tribe's winter camp. He pointed out the landmarks and told heartwarming stories about his experiences and the people he'd met in each of the places he'd been. Sometimes he simply used the markers as a reminder to pray for one of the people he ministered to.

The man cared for his flock, no doubt. Both the spiritual needs and their daily challenges, it seemed, with all these supplies he'd purchased to give to the tribe. This little band of Northern Peigan were luckier than they knew.

CHAPTER 9

Among these innocents is the one place I feel free.
~ Joseph's Journal

The children appeared first.

Monti had to bite back a cry when two miniature versions of the Indian braves they'd seen days before stepped around a rocky cliff onto the trail just ahead of them. The boys couldn't have been more than seven or eight, but they stood motionless, their faces stoic masks, devoid of any soft expression.

Until Antoine spoke some kind of gibberish to them. The smaller boy broke his stance first, his face spreading into a grin to match any carefree lad in Montreal. The taller one smiled, too, but seemed to be fighting it.

They strode forward, and soon a host of little figures surrounded their horses.

Antoine dismounted and spoke to the children, and Monti slid from her horse, as well. Her muscles still ached from so many days in the saddle, and she had to bite back a groan as her weary ankles complained about the need to hold her weight.

When she turned to face the clamoring voices, Joseph was by her side. She glanced up at him. Would he be tense and wary around the Indians?

His mouth was set in an amused tip as he watched the children. His lips spread into a full grin as a young girl approached him shyly.

He dropped to her level, sitting on his heels as she spoke to him. He responded in the same Indian tongue, then reached inside his coat and extracted something. When he held out his right hand, a peppermint stick sat on his palm.

The girl's eyes sparkled, and she stepped close enough to take the treat. She seemed to know Joseph, although shyness still lingered in her actions. Instead of taking the candy and darting backwards. She placed the confection in her mouth and beamed at Joseph around the stick.

He tweaked her ear and spoke to her again. His deep tenor held a teasing lilt.

The girl sidled closer, coming to a stop when she was close enough to touch Joseph's shoulder. With her hand resting there, she studied him. Not speaking, just seemingly content to suck her treat and watch to see what he might do next.

He spoke to her again, and she nodded. Then he scooped up the girl and held her in his right arm.

When he turned to Monti, the child beamed at her. "Monti, this is Hollow Oak." He looked at the girl and pointed to Monti. "Monti."

The child, who couldn't be more than three or four years old, looked at her. "Mon-ti." The little girl's words were precious.

Monti stroked the girl's arm. "It's a pleasure to meet you, Hollow Oak."

The girl turned to look at Joseph and giggled, as though tickled by the fact that Monti had spoken to her. Joseph tapped her nose and grinned wider than Monti had ever seen him. But who couldn't smile at that adorable little tawny face?

As they neared the Indian camp, Monti took in the teepees, which rose like steeples toward the clouds. More imposing than she'd imagined from Antoine's accounts. People milled around the area, women with long braids hanging over each shoulder and babies strapped to their backs. Men with equally long braids, working outside of the opened flaps of their homes.

Everyone stopped and watched them, and a single man strode forward to meet them just outside the circle of tents. He moved with a lithe grace, his bearing tall and regal. The children shifted from their cluster around Antoine to stand behind the Indian as though drawn to his magnetic leadership.

Antoine spoke to the man in the lyrical Indian tongue, and he responded in kind. It would have been nice to understand what was being said.

She stepped closer to Joseph and spoke under her breath. "What are they saying?"

"Just a greeting," he murmured back. "This is Hungry Wolf, chief of the village." Joseph paused. "And now the priest is introducing you."

She'd gathered as much when Antoine motioned back at them and spoke her name.

"Now he's telling about the supplies we brought."

The Indian nodded, then motioned at the village behind him and spoke a few syllables. His voice was decisive in its finality, and he turned and strode through the crowd of children as they parted for him.

"He said to go and do." Joseph turned to the horses and gathered their reins. "So I reckon' we'd best get started."

She stayed close to Joseph and Antoine as they distributed blankets and beads and food supplies to the people. They seemed to know her cousin well, and he joked with some of them, using a mixture of English and the Indians' language.

She couldn't help but notice one man who kept to himself, standing in front of a teepee at the edge of the group. His clothing was a bit more elaborate than the others, with bone and colored beadwork adorning his buckskin tunic. He wore some kind of feathered ornament in his hair, and most of the time he stood with his arms crossed, watching them.

"Who is he?" she asked Antoine as they left a group of young women and moved toward a circle of older women around a campfire.

"The Shaman. Medicine man. He's been hesitant to accept my presence among his people. His role is both healer and spiritual guide, and he questions the Good News I bring about our Lord."

The way the man's gaze seemed to penetrate was unnerving, yet part of her wanted to turn and speak to him. Just to face his scrutiny and prove she wasn't afraid of him. Even though the idea did make her heart race into her throat.

After visiting with the old squaws for a few moments, Antoine bid them farewell and continued on. She hadn't seen Joseph for a little while, and she scanned the area.

A group of children darted about on the hillside at the edge of the village, drawing her gaze that direction. A larger, buckskin-clad figure lunged forward, scooping up one of the little ones. The echo of a giggle rang across the distance, intermingled with a man's deep laugh.

She stared at the pair, the happy sounds seeping through her like a warm tea. Before she made the decision to step forward, her feet had already moved toward the gathering of playmates.

As she neared and the features of each became clear, she had to work to reconcile this picture of Joseph—playing with the Indian children, rolling on the ground in a mock wrestling match, tossing little Hollow Oak in the air until her giggles rang out. Was this the same Joseph she'd come to know over the past week? The man who'd been so quiet and somber?

This Joseph seemed to have lost the cloak of despair that sometimes shrouded him. This Joseph was light and carefree as a man enjoying the gifts God set before him.

He seemed to realize her presence then and turned to meet her gaze. The twenty feet or so that separated them melted away, and she lost herself in the twinkle of his amber gaze, the laugh lines around his eyes, the strength that resonated there.

She obeyed the magnetic pull that drew her toward him, but finally broke eye contact when Hollow Oak reached for her.

"Monti." The child's chubby hands reached around her neck as Monti took her, breathing in the warmth and softness of the little girl.

"Hello." She balanced the girl on her hip and looked into those dark eyes. Her face was smudged with dirt, and she seemed to be breathing hard. Monti glanced at Joseph. "I think you've worn her out."

He reached out and tugged one of the child's braids, then spoke in her language.

The girl snuggled into Monti's chest and looked at him shyly as she gave a soft answer.

He tapped her nose with a smile, then looked up at Monti. "She says she's hungry."

Monti tucked the girl in tighter, wrapping her arms around the little one. "We need to feed you then. What about the rest of the children? Are they all hungry?"

Joseph spoke the same words to them he'd asked Hollow Oak, and received a chorus of matching answers. He turned back to her with his mouth quirked. "Sounds like yes."

Together, they strolled with the children through the camp, and Joseph stopped them in front of a large fire pit where two women worked. When he spoke, she was finally able to pick out a series of sounds that matched what he'd said before.

"Áóoyiwa." Or something like that.

One of the women nodded and motioned toward a large carved wooden bowl. The children surged toward the dish, all reaching in and pulling out handfuls of some kind of mush. Apparently, it served as the village porridge bowl. At least for the children.

Hollow Oak squirmed, and Monti put her down, then stepped back beside Joseph as the girl scampered to join the others with their snack.

He touched her elbow. "I see the priest standing by the horses. We should get a move on before daylight leaves us."

The sun had been bright today, warming the air and softening the snow into trickles of water. She walked beside him, glancing around at the Indian camp that didn't seem quite as frightening now. But how different would it feel without the man striding beside her?

A strong part of her didn't want to know. Although soon she'd find out. Joseph had his own life to live, and she couldn't rely on him to be her crutch. Soon, she'd have to find the strength within herself to face her fears alone.

No, not alone. With God's help, she could accomplish anything.

$\sim$

*J*oseph reined in at the Bergeron cabin two days later, his ears picking up a scraping sound from around the side. He eased down from his saddle and moved toward the noise. Was the priest building something in the lean-to? It seemed a touch early in the day for that, but perhaps he needed to finish his work before they went back to the Indian camp.

As he stepped around the corner of the cabin, he stopped at the sight of a willowy backside. A familiar frame bending away from him as she scraped something out of a shallow pan. From the stench wafting toward him, she must have burned breakfast. Not surprising, since she had to cook over a hearth fire. Probably a task she'd never attempted back in Montreal.

He marveled at how far this French princess had come yet knew she'd mastered not even a fraction of what she had left to learn.

Which reminded him—he'd planned to teach her a few more meals. Now was probably as good a time as any.

He leaned against the corner of the house, propping one toe and crossing his arms over his chest. She made such a fetching image no matter what she did, and just now, it was hard to take his eyes from her.

It didn't take his conscience long to push through, though, so he spoke up to make his presence known. "Have you tried oat pudding yet?"

She whirled to face him, raising her wooden spoon as though she planned to use it like a club. When she got a good look at him, her body seemed to sag with relief. "Joseph, you scared the breath out of me."

He tried to hold in the grin that fought for release, but he couldn't quite control the corners of his mouth. "Sorry." Although, he might not have meant that apology as much as he should have.

"You are not." She blew at a piece of hair that clung to her mouth.

How did she know him so well already? His fingers itched to step forward and brush the hair from her face. But he forced himself to stay put. Maybe if he kept his focus on the cooking… "So what do you say? Oat pudding?"

She glanced down at the blackened pan in her hand. "My corn cakes didn't do so well this morning."

"I saw a barrel of oats under one of the crates in there, and I'm sure there're some dried onions and greens somewhere." He pushed off from the wall and reached for the pan. "It's one of the easiest meals I know, and a good change from corn mush."

She nodded and let him take the cast iron pan, then he followed her inside.

As they started into the simple meal, he was once again reminded how intelligent she was, easily catching onto ideas. And although she didn't know the names of many ingredients or cooking techniques he mentioned, once she understood the concept, she worked through chopping the greens and packing the boiling bag with a confidence not many new cooks would possess.

When they had the pudding in the cloth and boiling in a pot full of water, he glanced around the room. "Where's Father Bergeron?"

She wiped her hands on her apron. "He's gone for a walk to commune with God. I planned to have the morning meal ready when he returned. How long will this take?"

He eyed it. "About an hour, usually. I hope he planned a long walk." And that would mean he had an hour with Monti. Alone. Was that good or bad? His body and mind seemed to war within him over the question.

She glanced at him as she lifted the apron over her head. "What are you doing here? Surely you didn't come just to enjoy my tasty meals."

It was hard to hold in a smile at that, but he did his best. "I told your cousin I would help transport a few more supplies. He has more than could be tied onto the back of your saddles, so I brought a pack horse."

She nodded and moved to the other side of the cabin. "I wondered how many trips it would take us to deliver all this. I've sorted through the crates and stacked all the supplies over here."

As he followed her, his gaze swept around the room. The place did look a little different. Cleaner, maybe? The simple cabin seemed to have more of a smile than before. Although that sounded ridiculous.

She spun to face him. "Where can I get more fabric? Is there a mercantile in the area? And I'd like a rug—a nice big, colorful mat for the floor."

He raised his brows at her. "The nearest trading post is a day's ride away. You should talk to Emma, though. She's got that kind of stuff everywhere. I think she probably has extra in trunks."

A longing came into her gaze. "Your sister?"

The way she said it made him feel like an unthoughtful cur. Of course she'd want to get acquainted with the women in the area. She'd been away from civilization for weeks now, maybe even months. And since Emma and Aunt Mary were the only women within a half day's ride, he should orchestrate the meeting.

He propped his hands at his waist and scuffed his boot on the wooden floor. "I should take you to meet her. My Aunt Mary, too. If they knew you were here, they'd have been over already."

A noise sounded on the stoop, and the door creaked open.

"I'll see when Father Bergeron can spare you."

"I cannot spare her. Not ever." The priest's humorous tone entered the room before he did. After pulling off his gloves, he cupped his hands around his mouth and blew. "Now what is it you need my cousin for?"

Joseph fought the burn climbing his neck at the question, but it was no use. "I thought she might like to meet my sister and aunt. I could see if they can come here if it's too much for Monti to go for a visit."

The priest waved a dismissive hand. "Tomorrow is perfect for Monti to visit. I must travel to the Blood tribe over the mountain, and 'tis best I travel alone this time. There has been much sickness among them."

"But Antoine"— Monti stepped forward—"if the people are ill, you'll need my help. This is what I came for."

He waved her words away. "These people do not take well to strangers. I have worked many years to be accepted in even a small way. Besides, it is the pox, which I have already been burdened with. You, ma fifille, have not, and it would be harmful for you to be exposed."

An image of Monti with her face covered with red lesions flickered in his mind, and he tightened his jaw against it. "That disease could kill you, Monti. You can't go. I can collect you right after breakfast. Or..." His mind spun to find an ingredient he could bring and teach her to cook. "Maybe I'll see a snowshoe hare or two along the way and come a mite earlier. Perhaps you'd even offer to feed me if I brought part of the meal."

She looked torn, turning thoughtful eyes to him. At last, she offered a weak smile. "Oui. I would be pleased to meet your sister and your aunt."

Her words brought a flood of relief that finally eased the tension in his body. At least she wouldn't be exposed to the dangers of smallpox. And if he'd also won an extra day in her presence, well...even better.

CHAPTER 10

My heart aches for this pain another bears. I must find a way to help this time.

~ Monti's Journal

Monti's second trip to the Indian camp proved another eye-opening experience. The children flocked around them again, absorbing as much attention as the three of them could offer.

The adults seemed to be a bit harder to win over. The women were polite but never approached or spoke unless answering a question. Of course, asking a question was almost impossible for Monti, although she learned a few gestures in their sign language as the day progressed. The men kept to themselves mostly, sitting near a campfire crafting arrows or some other kind of wood carving. One of the men was carving bowls identical to the ones in Antoine's cabin.

She really wanted to examine the carvings closer but didn't dare stop and stare at the Indian braves. What would they think of that?

Joseph had left them before the midday meal, such as it was. Some kind of bread pudding that had steeped beside the fire several hours, then was allowed to form a crust on top. The taste wasn't so bad. Certainly better than the charred corncakes she'd tossed out that morning. Almost as good as the oat pudding Joseph helped her make.

He was such a conundrum. Both a tough mountain man and a competent cook. The same hand that strummed a guitar frequently killed and skinned wild animals. Had he learned his domestic skills from his sister? Possibly from living on his own, too. Monti was looking forward to meeting this twin sister, his closest family.

A touch on her elbow broke through Monti's thoughts, and she turned to see the pleasant face of a young Indian squaw. The woman spoke with a smile and motioned for Monti to follow her.

Monti glanced around for Antoine, but he was nowhere to be seen. Whatever this woman wanted, it would be helpful to have someone to translate for them. It appeared they'd have to muddle through with hand gestures.

She followed the lithe form of the young squaw to a teepee, and the woman motioned her to come inside as she stepped through the slit in the covering that served as a door.

Monti hesitated, glanced behind her. She'd not been inside one of the structures. Was it safe to enter alone? No sign of Antoine. If the Indians had planned to scalp her, they would have done so by now, right? And the woman might perceive it as an insult if she refused her hospitality.

Squaring her shoulders, Monti pulled one side of the opening back and peered in. The place seemed empty except the Indian woman, who was bent over something on the right. Monti stepped inside, and the woman motioned her over.

It didn't take long for her eyes to adjust to the dim interior, because light spilled through the fibers of the animal skins stretched tight. A fire danced in the middle of the structure, fighting off the chill and making the space smoky, but still rather cozy.

Monti approached the squaw, and a flicker of movement made her realize the woman knelt beside a person lying under a fur blanket.

"Monti."

She stepped nearer, and her heart squeezed at the sight of the little girl tucked in the covers. "Hollow Oak. What's wrong?" She looked to the squaw. "Is she napping?" Perhaps the girl was still small enough to need a midday rest.

The Indian's face was blank, so Monti pressed her hands together and laid her head against them as if she were sleeping. "Is she napping?"

The woman shook her head and pressed a fist to her chest, over her heart. She spoke something, but Monti had no idea what. Then she made a motion of breaking something with her hands.

Heart breaking? Heart hurting?

Monti looked to the girl again, dropping to her knees beside the pallet of animal skins. "What's wrong, *mon chou*? Are you ill?" She took Hollow Oak's hand as the woman—her mother?—stepped back to allow them space.

The girl's eyes seemed weak, and Monti pressed her free hand to one of her tawny cheeks. Not feverish, but her breathing seemed loud for such a small child. As though she struggled for each inhale.

She stroked the glossy black hair, softer than she would have expected. Hollow Oak's eyes drifted partway closed, and Monti kept stroking. Her breathing didn't seem to come any easier. What could be wrong with the girl? She'd been playing with Joseph and the others only an hour or so before. Some sort of running game where one person ran around and tagged the others, making them stand frozen until another person came and tagged them again.

Monti had watched from a distance while she followed Antoine on his rounds to visit people sitting in front of their lodges. Hollow Oak had seemed to be as vibrant as any young girl during the sport. But this wheezing definitely wasn't normal.

Perhaps she had a bad cold. Monti scanned her face for signs of leaking nose or other irritants. Truthfully, she looked well, save the insipid look to her eyes and the labored breathing.

Monti forced her mind to think back through the medical books she'd read through the years. Most had been on the workings of the heart and blood vessels. Many afflictions could cause difficulty breathing, she knew, but a heart not working at full capacity wouldn't be able to carry the oxygen the body required.

That likely wasn't the cause, but just in case, she ran her hand down the covers where they barely rose over the girl's legs. "I'm going to look at your feet, Hollow Oak." The child probably couldn't understand her, but perhaps talking would keep her from being surprised at the action.

The girl gave a groggy "hmm" but seemed to be almost asleep, so Monti moved slowly as she pushed the covers back to reveal the lower part of her leg.

The sight there formed a knot in Monti's midsection. Puffy ankles spread into swollen feet. Certainly not the way a four-year-old child's feet should look.

She turned back to the squaw, meeting her somber gaze. The way the woman had pressed her fist against her heart, then made the sign of something breaking. Did she know the girl's heart wasn't working correctly? How could she? Only a few highly-focused internal physicians understood the workings of the heart and pulmonary system. And although they could often properly diagnose a patient based on the symptoms and other medical details, there was no way to treat most heart or arterial conditions.

She'd seen so many sketches, some even colored with oils to show proper coloring, she could practically imagine this sweet child's internal pulmonary system as if it lay atop her skin. All the veins and arteries weaving through her body, working to feed blood, oxygen, and other nutrients to organs and limbs. Yet something in the region of her heart wasn't working as God intended.

Monti replaced the covers on Hollow Oak's legs and shifted to look at the child's chest where her heart struggled even now. *Lord, heal this child's body, just as you healed Jairus's daughter. Show me what I can do to help. Grant me wisdom, Father.*

She scanned the recesses of her mind for something that might benefit the girl. None of the elixirs she'd read about in the medical journals would be available out here. It seemed she'd heard of some kind of pepper that, when ground, would increase blood flow.

Perhaps there were other foods or herbs that could build up the nutrients and oxygen in the blood so the minimal amount the child's heart was able to pump would provide the most help for the body. Not treating the cause of the problem, but hopefully making the wee one more comfortable. And possibly stemming further complications.

Monti stroked the girl's hair one last time, then leaned forward and pressed a kiss to her forehead. "Rest easy, mon chou."

The words seemed to pull a memory from Monti's mind, stalling her before she straightened. For a small moment, she could hear another voice saying that same phrase. Calling to her, a voice from her past. The same gentle baritone in a rolling French cadence. Papa had spoken those words to her that last day. The evening when he'd tucked her into bed. He'd been breathing hard that night, also.

She'd begged for another story, one complete with lively accents told in a way only he could perform. He'd just begun a tale about a young French maiden when he gripped his left shoulder. His face had blanched white, and she'd tugged his hand.

"What's wrong, Papa?"

He'd gurgled a noise. Trying to answer her. Trying to tease in the easy way he always did to set things to rights.

Still clutching his shoulder, he collapsed onto her bed.

"Papa, tell me what's wrong. Papa, please." No matter how much she begged, he couldn't seem to speak to her.

At last, he turned to look at her, his eyes turning a dusky gray like those of an old man. She could see the love in them, the worry. Somehow she knew, in her five-year-old heart, she knew.

She'd lost him. Collapsing over his body, she sobbed and sobbed, clinging to her papa's hand.

Until Mama arrived, took Monti into her arms. They cried together.

The memories had been stuffed down so long, reliving them now brought a new burn to Monti's throat.

She turned away from Hollow Oak. This sweet girl wasn't her papa. Monti tried to summon a smile for the mother. "I'm going to find the priest. We'll get medicine for her." She should touch the woman's shoulder, squeeze her hand, somehow show the support of one woman reaching out to another. But she didn't have the strength just now.

Reliving the memories had taken too much from her. And yet, she'd sworn all those years ago those memories would never steal from her again. That's why she'd spent so much time learning about the human heart. Why she'd subscribed to the London Medical Journal since she was ten years old.

Never again would she be in a situation where she had to watch someone she loved die. Not if she had breath left to save them.

~

*M*onti wasn't ready when Joseph appeared on their doorstep the next morning.

She'd been up for two hours. Had fed the horses and the cluster of chickens Antoine kept in the lean-to. Made coffee, attempted biscuits, which she'd ended up feeding to the chickens, and scoured the floor. For some reason, her nerves were in a tizzy over today's visit.

Antoine had left on his morning walk but had been gone long enough that she expected him back any minute.

And now she stared at Joseph as he stood at the cabin doorway. "Come in." It was the only polite thing to say, but a part of her wanted to send him back on his merry way.

He held up a leather-wrapped bundle. "I brought breakfast. Hope you're hungry."

Her stomach chose that moment to gurgle in a most uncivilized manner. She tried to be discreet as she pressed a hand to her middle, but the damage had been done.

A twinkle shone from his eye, and a grin tugged at the corners of his mouth. "It seems I'm just in time."

She couldn't help her own grin as she stepped aside and motioned toward the table. "Does this food come already cooked or are we allowed the honors?"

That grin tugged harder at his lips. "I wouldn't deny you the pleasure. You should know me by now." After setting the bundle on the table, he motioned toward it. "I'll even let you open the gift."

She had to smile at that. She stepped forward to do as he'd said. How much of that particular honor was due to the struggle he'd have unwrapping the package with only the fingers of his right hand?

He'd still not mentioned his injury. Not even hinted about it. The longer she waited to ask about it, the more sacred the subject seemed to be. Maybe today, since it seemed they'd be spending a fair amount of time together. Hopefully, the opportunity would present itself for her to ask in a natural way.

When she pulled the leather back, two raw chunks of meat stared up at her. Some kind of liquid pooled under the hunks, and a tangy odor wafted up to her. She wouldn't quite say the contents smelled bitter, but the sight and stench were enough to make her stomach churn. "What are they?"

"I promised snowshoe hare. Now, there are plenty of ways to cook fresh meat. We could boil it, of course, and make a stew. But that takes time, and stew seems a waste for fresh meat, since it does such a good job covering up the flavor. We could roast it, but that takes even longer. Hare pie is always an option, but I think broiling might be the best for these. What say you?"

She tried to meet his gaze, but this new teasing side of Joseph had her a bit off-kilter. "I say, yes."

He nodded, then pulled a knife from the sheath at his belt. "Cut the meat into strips about an inch thick while I ready the fire."

He was a patient teacher, explaining how important it was for the flames to be smokeless, which was best accomplished when the logs were burnt about halfway through. By the time she had the meat prepared, he pronounced the gridiron hot enough.

"I'll just rub a bit of this grease on the bars so the meat doesn't stick." He knelt beside the hearth, his strong profile outlined by the firelight behind him. He seemed so sure of himself. She wasn't certain if she was more *impressed* by his endless abilities or *envious* of them.

The thought made her jerk her gaze from him. *I'm sorry, Lord.* Envy would be better channeled into the effort required to learn these skills herself.

They'd just spread the meat over the gridiron when the door opened and Antoine entered. He seemed more hunched than usual, with his thick animal skin coat and his walking stick.

He returned Joseph's greeting with a nod and a curious smile. "I see I am just in time to break the fast. We are thankful for your kindness to us, Joseph." That was the first time he'd used Joseph's first name.

She couldn't help but add, "Yes, we're all thankful you've saved us from my burnt biscuits."

He glanced at her with raised brows. "You attempted biscuits? That's not even something I would try to make over an open fire. Emma makes great biscuits in her oven. Maybe she'll have good advice."

Monti turned to clear the table in preparation for eating. Joseph spoke of his sister as though she had mastered everything. A woman above all others. Monti was slowly beginning to dread her meeting with this bastion of domestic ability.

CHAPTER 11

Why art thou cast down, O my soul? and why art thou disquieted in me?
Hope thou in God.
~ Monti's Journal

As Monti poured coffee and set out plates for the meal, Antoine shuffled around in the corner where he kept his personal belongings.

Now would be a good time to talk through their plans for the day. "How far away is the tribe you're going to see?"

He kept working as he answered. "A half day's ride over the mountain."

A niggle of alarm tugged in her chest. "Is it safe to travel back after dark?"

"*Non.* I shall stay the night with the Blood people and return by the morrow's eve." He turned his focus to her. "Perhaps it would be best for you to stay the night with Madame Grant. She would welcome your presence, I am sure."

She opened her mouth to object, but Joseph stepped into the

conversation. "Emma will want you to stay. You won't be safe here alone."

She spun on him. "I'll be perfectly safe. I haven't even met your sister. I'll not foist myself upon her as a houseguest at our first acquaintance."

Normally, men stepped away from the glare she aimed at him. It was the same look Mama had perfected to aid her in business negotiations.

Joseph stepped closer, though, bringing him near enough she could smell that scent that had come to mean strength and safety to her.

His voice lowered, its timbre sinking through her chest. "You don't have to, Monti. But maybe keep it as a possibility. Wait until you meet my family, then decide."

She stared into those amber eyes, darkened by the dim lighting in the cabin, yet still bright enough to shine through to her very soul. "All right." The words came out just above a whisper as she forced them around the tightness in her throat.

His mouth formed a soft curve, then he broke their gaze, looking toward the fire. "It smells like our breakfast might be ready."

⁓

*J*oseph struggled for something to say as the silence stretched on during their ride. It wasn't like Monti to lack for words, and the tight line of her normally soft mouth made it clear she was nervous. She had no reason to worry, of course. Emma would adore her. Hannah, too. And Simeon would go along with whatever Em decided, although he'd probably share Joseph's concern about a young, unprotected woman surviving alone in these parts. But Monti seemed nervous about meeting his family no matter how much he'd assured her, and the longer they rode, the tighter she gripped her saddle horn.

"We'll see the house once we reach the top of that rise." He motioned toward a gentle swell in the snowy ground.

She offered only a stiff nod. Apparently, he'd not said the right thing to ease her nerves.

Maybe he could distract her. "How did things go with Hungry Wolf's people after I left yesterday?"

She darted an almost surprised look at him. "All right, I suppose. Except...did you know something is wrong with Hollow Oak's heart?"

"Wrong? You mean she's sick? She seemed to be running and playing fine while I was there."

As Monti told of Flying Dove calling her into their teepee, then seeing the child struggling for breath as she slept, her tone took on a deeper urgency with each sentence. "Her feet were so swollen. Something is stopping her heart from pumping the blood effectively."

He tipped his head at her as his mind scrambled to catch up with her flow of thinking. Maybe he'd been too focused on how upset she was and not paying enough attention to her words. "How do you know it has anything to do with her heart? Maybe she just has a childhood ailment that will go away in a few days."

She shook her head before he even finished his words. "I've seen this. I've studied the workings of the heart and circulatory system for years. Something isn't working correctly, and her mother knows it too."

Too many questions assailed him, but he honed in on the one most curious. "You've been studying the workings of the heart for years? How...why?" What would possess a young woman to study medicine of that nature?

Her face seemed to harden. Or maybe just grow more stubborn. "Because I wanted to. But I don't know what we can do for Hollow Oak. There's been much discovery about heart conditions, especially genetic disorders that affect children. But none of the physicians working in that field have uncovered what can be done to save a child still living."

He let her words sink in, sorting them from one angle, then another. "Simeon might be able to help. He knows all kinds of plants and herbs that are good for healing. Even saved my life once or twice with them. We can ask him."

Her dainty brows pulled together as though she weren't sure what to think about his offer. "I suppose it couldn't hurt. I spoke with Antoine, but his only advice was prayer. Which I've done, of course."

They were mounting the rise then, and Monti's attention was drawn to the valley that stretched out before them. The ground was vast and mostly open, as large in footprint as a mountain. Sprawling enough that Aunt Mary's ranch existed in the same basin as Simeon and Emma's cabin, but you could barely see one from the other.

From the side they entered, Monti would see the cabin perched about halfway across the valley before them. A cozy structure, with a barn and fenced pens scattered around the house.

Joseph could picture the scene in his mind, yet that wasn't what took up his thoughts just now. He couldn't quite pull his gaze from Monti's face. The look of awe brightening her dainty features made her features almost glow. Perhaps that was the sun still low in the eastern sky, but no matter the reason, she looked more like an angel than any creature he'd ever seen.

Breathtaking.

She turned to him then, catching him staring, locking her gaze with his. Her eyes shimmered in a kind of joy that seemed to radiate from her very soul. Something inside him reached out to her, wanted to touch her. He had to fist his good hand around the saddle to keep from pulling her horse close and following through with his body's yearning.

A soft smile touched her eyes first, slipping down to take over all her features. Then she glanced back at the valley before them and nudged her mare forward. "It looks like we're almost there."

As she rode forward, her words seemed to reverberate in his chest. *Almost there.* If only. But he didn't let himself linger long enough to think how nice it might be if they were almost to a home they shared, this woman filling it with her angelic presence.

～

*M*onti had prepared herself for any number of possible meetings with Joseph's family—especially his sister. Maybe Emma would be plain and shy. Perhaps she would be curly-haired and outgoing. Mayhap tall and winsome. She had to be an excellent homemaker, because Joseph seemed to hold her up as one of the most able domestics in the land. How much of that was brotherly affection and how much was truth?

The woman whose face lit when she opened the cabin door had to be Joseph's sister. She had the same coffee-colored hair and the same striking reddish-brown eyes. "Come in, please."

Joseph motioned for Monti to precede him into the house. "Emma, this is Miss Monti Bergeron." He motioned toward her, but before he could finish his introduction, his sister took hold of Monti's arm.

"I can't tell you how happy I am to meet you. Joseph's told us so much about you. It's about time he finally brought you here."

Monti had planned to curtsey as was a proper greeting, but Emma's lively welcome pulled her off-course. He'd told them so much about her? "The pleasure is mine, Madame Grant."

"Emma, please. We're not so formal in this part of the country. You must be freezing. Come to the fire and warm yourself. I have mulled cider warming, would you like some?" She sent an affectionate smile at her brother. "Joseph will drink it all if I let him, so you'd best have your fill now."

Monti removed her gloves and accepted the mug of cider, letting its spicy scent waft through her. Although Emma seemed eager to chatter, she had a kind of humble graciousness that emanated from her with every word and expression.

"Where's my sidekick?" Joseph accepted his own mug from his sister as he stood by the fire.

"Napping, but she'll probably hear your voice and be up any minute."

Joseph shot Monti a mischievous look. "Can I wake her up then?"

"You certainly cannot." Emma glared at him, then sent Monti a long-suffering smile. "He doesn't realize how precious naptime can be. I get more done in that one hour than I do all afternoon."

Joseph said, "You'd get more done if you didn't play so much."

Emma just shook her head. "Speaking of work, I was preparing dumplings for the midday meal. Monti, would you like to roll the pastry for me? I'm hoping Joseph will split more wood small enough to fit in the cook stove."

"I just get here and she's already putting me to work." He shook his head as if he were disgruntled. But the look he slid Monti showed his humor.

"It's about time you earn your keep around here." She looked at him with a bemused expression as he headed toward the door.

"Where's Simeon hiding out?" He stopped to refasten the buttons on his coat.

"He's gone to check the horses, but he'll be back to eat with us."

The door closed behind Joseph, shutting away the outside sounds and settling a quiet over the room. Emma turned a kind smile on her. "I don't mean to put you to work, too. Just sit at the table and visit while I finish this."

Monti stepped toward the kitchen. "No, please. I'd like to learn your recipe for dumplings." Not that she had her own recipe or anything, but she'd rather not let this woman know exactly how inept she was in the kitchen. Unless Joseph had told her.

She followed Emma toward the cookstove and work counters.

"It's hard to get supplies out here, but Simeon makes a run to town every few weeks for whatever they have in. As long as he can get flour, we're able to grow or hunt most everything else we—"

A bang at the door cut her short, and they both whirled to face the sound. Emma moved that direction, but had only taken a step when the door flew open.

A large man in a thick animal-skin coat barged in, something furry cradled in both arms.

"Simeon." Emma was by his side in a second. "What's happened?"

The man turned to his wife, giving Monti a better view of his front. He carried some kind of grayish-colored dog that had a bright spot of crimson marring the hair on its side. The blood dripped down from the animal in a steady stream, pooling on the cabin floor.

"Wolves...after the horses." He struggled to catch his breath. "When I got there, they were after the black mare. Mustang chased them off, but he took a beating."

Emma leaned close over the dog's head. "Hey, boy." Then she stepped back. "I'll get a blanket and the medicine box. There's water heating by the fire."

Mr. Grant glanced around, his gaze coming to rest on her. He nodded, then moved toward the hearth.

Monti turned toward Emma. "What can I do?"

She motioned toward the counter. "There's a crate under there with bandages and dried herbs and such. Take that to Simeon while I get a blanket."

Monti found the box, then turned to the man and dog on the other side of the room. They'd not even been introduced, but it seemed formality really didn't have much place here on the frontier. Squaring her shoulders, she strode over to him.

He looked up from where he seemed to be examining the animal's wounds. "You must be Miss Bergeron."

"Yes." She dipped in a slight curtsy. Something about the man seemed so daunting. Not that he was frightening, per se, but he seemed to have a wild aura about him. As though he'd been carved from the mountains that stood as sentries around this valley.

She knelt by the dog's feet, placing the box where the man could reach it. "What next?"

"Bring that water over here. And I'll need a rag. Maybe you can find one by the sink."

She did as he asked, finding a cloth that looked dry and unused. As she moved back toward the wounded animal, the cabin door swung open again. Joseph stepped inside, and the sight of him loosened the knot clenched in her chest.

His gaze met hers. "What's wrong? I saw Simeon's horse and a trail of blood."

She motioned toward the man and dog, then proceeded in that

direction. "The dog is hurt. He said wolves attacked the horses." She knelt again and handed the cloth to Simeon, who pressed it against the dog's side where the blood seemed to be coming in a steady flow.

Joseph knelt behind her, his presence both soothing her nerves and awakening a riot of butterflies in her middle. He was close enough she could feel his warmth, even though he didn't touch her.

"Anyone else get hurt?" His voice rumbled near her ear. If she turned to look at him, their faces would likely be less than a foot apart.

But she didn't turn.

"One of the broodmares. I think she's all right, but I need to get back out and check her. Make sure they don't come back to finish the job." Simeon's attention drew upward to a point behind them, a bit of relief slipping over his face.

Monti turned to see Emma approaching. She held up a gray woolen blanket and moved around to sit in front of the dog. "Have you washed it yet?" She spoke in a low tone, her words obviously meant for her husband.

"Just staunching the blood."

"Do you need to get back to the horses?" She looked up at him, studying his face with twin lines furrowing her brow.

He nodded, his gaze shifting between her and the dog. "I would use the powdered pepper first, then we'll try comfrey tonight."

"That's what I was thinking, too."

Their gazes locked, and something intimate passed between them. She found herself watching Simeon's face, which looked—thankful? Relieved? As if all would be better with Emma's help.

She knew that feeling. The startling realization made her pull back a bit. The look on Simeon's face was exactly how she felt when Joseph had walked into the room moments ago.

She wanted to dart a glance at him, but her spinning mind wouldn't let her. What did it all mean? Thankfully, she didn't have long to ponder, because Simeon rose to his feet, towering over them.

Joseph stood, too. "I'll help with the horses."

She wanted to protest, ask him not to leave her here. She'd almost rather go help tend the horses and fight off wolves if it meant Joseph would be with her. But a look at Emma stilled her racing heart.

"We'll take care of things here." Emma spoke to the men but kept her calming amber eyes on Monti. As though she could read her impulsive desire.

Monti inhaled a steadying breath and nodded. She was a Bergeron. She didn't need a man to lean on. Especially not when someone—or something, in the case of this poor dog—needed her.

CHAPTER 12

These questions have turned to a battle inside me.
~ Joseph's Journal

*M*onti worked with Emma to tend the dog, at least for the first few minutes. The animal had several deep gashes across its side and abdomen, and a chunk of flesh hung loose from one front leg. The wounds were hard to look at, but the way the dog gazed up at her, its tongue lolling to the side, made her want to stay with him and ease away the pain.

"He's usually not good with new people, but he seems to like you." Emma watched the animal as Monti stroked its head.

"He must hurt a great deal." The dog's coarse hair bounced back up after each time her hand passed over it.

"That tea we gave him should help. Even in pain, though, Mustang doesn't take to people easily. I think he only tolerates my presence because of Simeon. And because I feed him." Her voice held a smile.

Monti used her thumb to stroke the bones just in front of the dog's ear. His eyelids drifted partway closed, and his panting turned into a contented sound.

"Yes," Emma said. "He's smitten. And he doesn't seem to be the only one."

Monti's gaze jerked up to the other woman. "What do you mean?"

But a baby's cry pierced the air, and Emma stood. "Hannah's awake."

Monti wanted to chase her, to question her further about what the woman meant. Surely she didn't see something between her and Joseph. There wasn't anything to see, except this unsettling need she seemed to have for his presence. A need she'd best obliterate...post haste. She'd never needed a man, and she didn't plan to start now.

A few minutes later, Emma returned with a cute girl on her hip, her brown curls splaying in all directions. The child's face was red and splotchy from her short bout of tears.

Emma brought her over. "Hannah, this is our new friend Miss Monti. Can you say, hello?"

The child dove into her mother's shoulder, taking refuge there as though she couldn't stand to meet a newcomer.

Monti reached up from her seat beside the dog and tweaked one of Hannah's little stockinged feet. "Hello, Hannah. It's a pleasure to meet you."

Emma tried to coax her daughter into a greeting, but Hannah kept her face pressed into her mother's shoulder. Emma finally sent Monti an apologetic smile. "She feels a bit overwarm. I think she may not be feeling well."

The next hour passed in a busy blur. Poor Hannah fussed off and on, especially when Emma tried to set her on the floor with her doll. Finally Emma gave up and bounced with the child as she swayed to and fro. Monti moved to the kitchen and helped as she could while Emma gave instruction on how to fold the dumplings, what to mix for the cream sauce, and how to shift it about on the stove top to keep the mixture from burning with the varying temperatures of the fire.

"That looks perfect," Emma finally proclaimed. "Now you can move the pot to the edge of the stove where it will only get enough heat to stay warm. Hopefully, the men will be back before it turns to mush."

Monti gave the mixture a final stir. It did look perfect and smelled just as good. Joseph would be shocked that she'd made more than corncakes without burning them.

Of course, she'd had Emma giving instructions the entire time.

Monti had just settled in beside Mustang again when a boot thud sounded on the stoop outside. The door pushed open, and Simeon stepped inside. Joseph followed him, and his gaze immediately scanned the room until it landed on her.

Or...maybe his gaze had been searching for the dog. She tried to offer a reassuring smile and speak as if that were the case. "He's staying calm, which is good. How are the horses?"

Joseph approached her and dropped to his knees, the animal between them. "The mare had some deep marks, but she should be all right. We brought her to the barn to keep an eye on her."

"And her foal? Will she have trouble?" What a horrible thing to happen with a young one on the way.

He looked up from the dog and met her gaze. "I hope not. Time will tell. She looks like she only has a couple months left." His eyes glimmered sadness, not the callused look of a man accustomed to such bloodshed.

"I hope you're all hungry. Monti made dumplings for the meal." Emma's voice broke through the haze that seemed to surround the two of them.

His eyes softened and crinkled at the edges. "Dumplings, eh?" His voice was low, his words for her alone. "I'm definitely hungry."

She couldn't speak. Couldn't breathe with the way he looked at her. What was it about this man that affected every part of her so strongly?

At last, he straightened, breaking the invisible connection that pulled at her. After standing, he held out his right hand to help her up. He still wore his gloves, although he'd unbuttoned his coat.

She placed her hand in his and allowed his strength to aid her as she rose. It might have been her imagination, but it seemed as if he gave her fingers a gentle squeeze before letting go. It was hard to be sure through his leather gloves, though. Was there a chance he felt more for her than kindness, or maybe even friendship? That must be what his sister had meant. But smitten? That was so far from possible, the idea was almost laughable. She wasn't the kind of woman Joseph needed. Not competent in this mountain wilderness. And besides, she's sworn off men. Ever since that day when she was fifteen, she'd vowed never to trust a man again. Mama hadn't needed a man, not after Papa died. And she didn't need one either.

She moved to the kitchen and dished out the food while Emma settled Hannah for the meal and the men washed up. The air had a cozy feel. Homey. As if they were all one big family. Which they were, she supposed. The others, anyway. She was the outsider here.

But as Emma asked Monti to hand her the cloth she tied around her daughter's neck to keep her clothes clean, and Joseph offered a gentle curve of his lips when she filled his coffee mug, she couldn't help but feel like part of their family.

She was accepted here. Among these people who'd absorbed her in their midst as though she'd always belonged.

$\sim$

*A*fter they ate, Joseph accompanied the rest of them to the barn to examine the wounds on the expectant mare. Monti had suggested she stay inside to finish cleaning the kitchen, but Emma wouldn't hear of it. And he was glad to be in her company again. He'd thought he'd spend the whole day with her, yet aside from dinner, he'd barely seen her since they'd arrived.

They neared the stall and found the mare in the corner, resting with one hind foot cocked. That resting leg was the one that had been pierced by the fangs of a wolf, and the injured area had already swelled.

Simeon applied a fresh dose of salve there and to the other lacerations. Emma brought in a bit more hay and coddled the girl for a few minutes. Even Monti stepped into the pen and stroked her dark winter coat. Joseph could only imagine what it was like to have her stroking and whispering sweet comforts in one's ear. He was having trouble summoning pity for the mare just now.

"Neigh-neigh." Hannah reached toward the horse, almost pulling herself out of his arms.

"You want to pet the horse?" He straightened the little mite and stepped into the enclosure with the others. The women eased back to give him room, and he helped his niece pet the mare, snuggle into her mane, and plant a kiss on her forehead.

"All right, ladybug. Bid her good day." He pulled Hannah back and stepped away.

"G'da." Hannah waved to the horse, and he couldn't help a grin.

He turned and caught Monti's gaze, sharing a smile with her. Who couldn't feel a bit happier when spending time with this little muffin?

~

The afternoon passed in a blur for Monti, especially when they all climbed into the Grants' sleigh and rode across the valley to visit with Joseph's aunt and uncle. Madame Lockman was a feisty woman with hair cropped almost as short as her husband's. The lady even wore men's pants, although the apron she tied over them while the women prepared dinner helped soften the shocking appearance a little.

Monsieur Lockman didn't often fit a word into the conversation, and at first he seemed extremely shy. His wife appeared to handle the talking for both of them. But as he leaned over and spoke to Madame in low French tones, realization slid over Monti. He might prefer listening over talking, but it probably had as much to do with not speaking English well as it did with personal preference.

As often as Monti could without seeming rude to the others, she slipped into French to communicate with him. He seemed eager to answer her questions about how long they'd lived in this part of the frontier, how many horses and cattle they owned, and whatever else she could think of.

She found herself seated beside Monsieur Lockman at the evening meal, which gave him the chance to tell her more about how they'd come to settle their ranch. He'd left France twenty years before—the same year Monti was born. After a horrid week in Quebec, he'd traveled on, first down the Ottawa River, then westward. The moment he'd seen the peaks of these Rocky Mountains, he said he'd finally found his home.

"Everything seemed perfect, especially after I met this lady, the love of my life." He leaned over to wrap an arm around Madame Lockman's shoulder.

She gave him a smile that was part chastisement, part adoration, then turned to Monti and said in the same French language. "I'd been living at the trading post over the mountain until my first husband left me a widow. Never would have stayed in the area if I hadn't met Adrien. Now I can't imagine leaving." They shared another look and smile that was...well, the English didn't seem to have a word sweet enough to describe the strength and staying power of the love that drifted between them. As though it had been tried by fire and come out stronger and purer.

She looked away, as much to give them privacy as to soften the ache in her chest the sight brought on. She'd never had the desire to marry. Mama had never seen the need to remarry and had done well for them both. When Monti made the choice to come west to this wilderness, she'd decided to become something of a nun. She was married to her Lord, here to carry out His will and spread His word.

Her gaze wandered to Joseph, as it did more than it should these days. He was already looking at her, and his gaze seemed to bore through her, so penetrating she couldn't pull herself from it. Yet he didn't seem to be studying her as much as just buried deep in his thoughts. His face held an odd expression. Intense. Was he irritated with her? Or maybe with something else. Yet... he didn't quite look angry. She couldn't identify what she found in his gaze.

She finally pulled her focus from him. The man was confusing enough sometimes to give one a headache.

Thankfully, Emma asked her aunt a question about their livestock, bringing a renewed lightness to the conversation and a fresh direction for Monti's frustrating thoughts.

She'd do well not to dwell on Joseph Malcom.

~

A war raged inside Joseph as he accompanied the others back to Emma's home. Watching her speak French with Uncle Adrien had awakened something inside him that wouldn't return to its dormant state.

She'd been beautiful. But that was nothing new. Every time he looked at her, he had to steel himself against her beauty. It was the gentle way she'd sought out his uncle, the man who'd learned to resign himself to the role of observer in most conversations. She'd gone out of her way to converse with him, and in so doing, had brightened both his aunt and uncle's day considerably, if he judged by the glow that now surrounded them.

Monti cared about people so much. It wasn't a trait he'd expected when he first met the French princess at Fort Hamilton. He'd assumed she would be ignorant and snobbish. It turned out she was strong and kind and braver than he could ever dream of being.

Which meant he was nowhere near good enough for her. He'd known that since the first day, although he'd not let his mind go anywhere near those thoughts. But now, he couldn't seem to stop himself from dwelling on the differences between them.

He was a cripple.

She was the most beautiful creature God created.

He was a roving wanderer. No real plans, if he were honest.

She'd traveled for weeks in uncivilized conditions to befriend and share her faith with people she'd never met. People considered by many to be savages.

Which brought him to the biggest difference. She believed God cared.

He didn't. At least, God didn't care for him.

When Simeon reined the team in at the cabin, Joseph motioned for him to climb down with the women. "I'll unhitch. I need to saddle my gelding, too. I'll come in to say goodnight before I head out."

"No, Joey. Stay the night with us." Emma's voice took on that big sister tone. Since she'd been born a handful of minutes before he had, she always seemed to think that made her the eldest and responsible for him. "You can't go up to your cave tonight, it's too late. We'll make a pallet for you in the main room."

He tried to summon a bit of teasing, but he didn't have it in him after fighting this internal battle all evening. "I told Uncle Adrien I'd stay there and help him brand calves first thing in the morning. You already have a houseguest you can fuss over."

She glanced toward the cabin, where Monti had already carried Hannah inside. Then she turned back to Joseph, her hand resting on the sleigh bench as she eyed him. "I like her, Joey. I really do. I'm glad you brought her."

He just nodded, not meeting Emma's gaze.

"Let's get in out of the cold, wife." Simeon wrapped an arm around her shoulders. Thank God this brother by marriage wasn't as pushy as his sister.

CHAPTER 13

My heart yearns, yet my mind fears.
~ Monti's Journal

Once Joseph had the horses inside the barn and the sleigh disconnected and pushed into place, he set about unhitching the animals. The buckles were frustrating to manage with only the fingers on his right hand.

For that matter, *everything* was frustrating to manage with only his right hand.

After working for a good two minutes on the buckle fastening the bridle on the bay gelding, his muscles over his shoulders had bunched in a tight yoke. He'd already jerked the glove off his right hand so his fingers could work better, but it wouldn't help any to take off the left one.

Nothing would ever make those fingers work better.

Finally, the strap came loose. He restrained the anger coursing through him long enough to remove the contraption from the horse's head. When the leather pulled free, he flung it on the ground by the nearest stall.

He did jerk the glove off his left hand then. White flesh glared up at him. The fingers small and curved. Hideous.

"Joseph?"

He whirled at the voice, tucking his useless hand behind him. Monti stood a few steps inside the barn, eyeing him. The hood of her coat framed her face, accentuating her delicate features.

His mouth went dry. Hopefully, she was too far away to have seen his hand. And the horses' necks might have shielded him. If he were lucky.

She stepped nearer, coming around the front of the horses, which waited patiently for the remaining harness to be removed. "Emma said you weren't staying the night. I don't want you to leave on account of me. They're your family, I can sleep on the floor behind a curtain or..." She looked around as though trying to find a suitable place in the barn.

He spoke up before she could offer anything so outlandish.

"I'll be helping my uncle with his branding early in the morning. It only makes sense for me to sleep over there. Don't trouble yourself." He didn't mean for his voice to sound so gruff, but the last thing he needed was her presence out here.

It'd be easier to remember how far out of his reach she was if he didn't have to be near her so much. The way she looked at him sometimes made him hope for things he had no right to want.

Like now. She studied him in that special way only she could master—a mixture of suspicion and softness. Like she cared, but didn't want to let herself get too close.

A wise choice.

But then she stepped forward, stopping when she was near enough that she could reach out and touch him if she wanted to.

He pressed his crippled hand behind him. "You should go back in where it's warm." He was being a cad, but he couldn't stop himself. He had to get away from her. For her own good.

"Joseph. Have I done something to anger you?" Her voice was soft and gentle. Alluring.

He swallowed, trying to force words through his parched throat. He couldn't seem to pull his gaze from her. "Of course not."

"That's good." She seemed to move nearer. Or maybe it was his imagination. His wretched hopes drawing her closer.

He turned away, careful to keep his left hand out of her sight.

"Are you hiding something?"

He jerked back, but her curiosity had been roused.

She peered as if trying to see behind him. "What is that?"

"Nothing." He didn't mind sounding terse this time. She needed to keep her nosy gaze to herself.

"What is it, Joseph. Are you hurt?" She stepped closer and grabbed his coat sleeve. "I can help."

He yanked his coat out of her hand. "Monti, I said it's nothing."

She stilled, her gaze wandering up to meet his. He'd wounded her. His words. His tone. Yet mixed with the hurt showing there, he caught a glimpse of stalwart determination.

"Joseph." Her voice lowered, gentled. "I know you've been injured. I've seen the scar. Is there something I can do to help?"

Her words slammed into him, leaving him swaying from their impact. How had she seen the scar? He never took his glove off. *Never.*

Before he realized what she was doing, she slipped her hand around his left arm, then ran her fingers down the length of it. Pulling free his hand. Drawing it into the light.

The white skin was almost blinding, the jagged red scar running across the back of his hand roiling nausea in the pit of his stomach. She held his hand in hers, running her thumb over the scar.

He tried to yank back, but she held his hand tightly. Yet gently.

His fingers hung over the edge of hers. Lifeless. They were touching her skin, yet he couldn't feel any of it. He had no power to control them. It had all been stolen away.

"What happened, Joseph?" She asked the question without looking at his face, just kept sliding the pad of her thumb back and forth over the bright red mark.

"An avalanche. Icy rocks loose in the snow. They came down on me. Pinned my hand for a while. Haven't been able to feel or use the fingers since." It must have been the entrancing effect of her thumb that released his tongue, dazed his mind. Even now, his thoughts felt as numb as his fingers. Frozen.

Her hand still enclosed his, but now, she slid it down to his fingers. His awful, white, limp fingers. Her thumb stroked across them once.

He should pull away. Should turn and leave this place. But he couldn't seem to drag himself from the trance of watching her skin move across his.

Then she raised his hand, turned hers so their palms met. Their fingers intertwined. If only he could feel it. As their fingers wove between each other, it was almost impossible to tell which were hers and which were his. They blended. A perfect match.

She looked up at his face then, and he met her gaze. He tried to prepare himself for the pity, but what he saw there shot fire to his very core.

Longing.

She rose up on her tiptoes, and he knew what she was doing. He wanted to pull back, but the part of him that had dreamed of this moment took over.

He met her hungrily, his good hand wrapping around her neck. Her hood fell away, and he worked his fingers into her hair. Her lips were warm and tender. Tentative, yet searching.

He absorbed the feel of her. The warm, almost exotic scent that swept through him to steal away his composure.

He'd longed for this touch more than he'd let himself acknowledge. And now, she seeped into him with a heady rush. He had to get control of himself before he lost all of himself to her.

With the last shreds of his strength, he pulled back. Just an inch, and their breathing mingled. Hers held such a tantalizing warmth, it threatened to pull him back in. So he withdrew further, this time enough that he could see her face. Her awe-inspiring beauty that had the power to drop him to his knees. Her eyes drifted open, lazily at first, then wider.

"Joseph." She whispered his name with part awe, part shock.

He had to war against himself to keep from pulling her back for another kiss. Instead, he swallowed. Forced himself to say what he had to. "I'm sorry." The words came out hoarse. "I shouldn't have done that. I…I'm sorry."

He couldn't think what else to say, but if he didn't get away from her now, he wasn't sure he'd be able to control himself much longer.

Reaching out, he pulled her hood back over her hair, allowing his thumb to trail the outline of her cheek as a final indulgence. So soft.

He met her gaze. "Go back inside, Monti."

After a final look of those dark fathomless eyes, she nodded, then turned and left the barn.

And as he watched her go, it felt as if she'd taken the last of his strength with her.

~

So many emotions swirled in Monti's chest, she had to stop and lean against the outside of the cabin to pull herself together before going in.

She'd just kissed Joseph. And what a kiss.

But how could she have? As much as she respected him, as safe as he made her feel, as much as his looks had captured her from the first time she'd met him, she'd not come to this place for romance.

She'd come to help people. To help Antoine and minister to the Indians. Maybe that was why she'd kissed Joseph. He'd looked so miserable as he told her about his injury. Had she kissed him in an impulsive attempt to help him feel better?

Her mind replayed the sensation of his mouth on hers, and a skitter slipped through her. No, that kiss had not been meant to ease his sadness. Or at least, not completely. She'd not realized how much she'd longed to touch him—maybe to kiss him, if the results were any indication. When she'd been so close, touching his hand, the kiss—it had all seemed the right thing to do.

Heat seared her cheeks. She had to get inside, but the last thing she wanted was Joseph's sister catching sight of her rumpled and flushed. She'd know what had happened, Monti would put money on it. Emma seemed to have an uncanny intuition when it came to things like that, especially where her brother was concerned.

Monti reached for the latch string and pushed the door open. Hopefully, she'd be able to slip into the bed chamber she'd been offered without too much notice.

~

*J*oseph didn't appear the next day.

Monti tried to focus on enjoying her new friends and learning what she could from Emma. Little Hannah made an excellent distraction, with her chubby smiles and the way she kept bringing her doll over for Monti to snuggle and make "talk."

It was just the three of them at the midday meal, as Simeon had gone to help with the branding, too. "How long does it normally take?" Monti asked as she raised a bite of stew to her mouth.

"I think they're just doing the new calves. Simeon seemed to think he'd be back in a few hours." Emma spooned a bite of potato into Hannah's mouth, then smiled at her daughter. "That's good isn't it?"

"Good." The little girl flashed a triumphant smile with the word. A grin one couldn't help but return.

Monti took another bite, her thoughts warring inside her as she debated whether to ask the question that had simmered inside her all morning and most of the night before. Perhaps it would be best to ask, so she would know the details. Emma surely wouldn't tell anything Joseph wouldn't want her to know.

She inhaled a solidifying breath. "Emma, can I ask about the accident that injured Joseph's hand?"

The other woman looked up for a moment, and her spoon hovered over the bowl. "I'm surprised he told you about that. He keeps it covered up and tries to pretend nothing happened."

How could she explain that she forced it out of him? "I asked him about it. He said he was caught in an avalanche and the hand was pinned under rock. How long was he trapped like that? Was he by himself?"

Emma let out a long sigh and sat back. "Unfortunately, yes. Simeon and I married as soon as we arrived in this part of the country, and from then on, Joseph became something of a wanderer. At first, I thought he was just excited to see the land, especially since he didn't have to worry about me any longer. And I think that was part of it. I didn't realize 'til later that he seemed to be struggling to put down roots."

She shrugged. "At least, I think that's what it is. I guess I'm still not really sure." She picked at the serviette in her lap, as though remembering scenes from the past. "Anyway, about four months ago, my uncle came racing over to our cabin. Said one of his men had found Joseph riding back from the mountains just north of here. Those peaks have snow all year round. Apparently, Joseph had been trying to climb to the top. Why he did it, I still can't tell you.

"Somehow, he started a small avalanche. It didn't bury him completely, but boulders came down with it and pinned his hand. He was stuck for almost an hour before he found a way to work himself loose. He said he thought about cutting his hand off to get away, but he couldn't quite bring himself to do it. Not yet, anyway."

Monti shivered at the thought, her eyes dropping shut as she imagined what it must have been like to be stuck on a mountain, half buried in the snow. His hand smashed and in worlds of pain. Miles from his family, and probably no one aware of where he was. He lived such a vagrant lifestyle, it might have been days before anyone missed him. And then where would they look?

She opened her eyes to Emma again. "What happened when he got loose?"

"He made it back to his horse. It's a wonder he didn't lose more than the feeling in that one hand." Her eyes glazed over. "It's a miracle, really. Only God could have saved him from frostbite up on that mountain."

"I agree." *And thank You, Lord, for keeping him safe.*

After several moments, Emma seemed to pull herself together.

"Anyway, the ranch hand found Joseph when he was out hunting for strays. Joseph must have been riding for several hours in those wet clothes. By the time they found him, he was almost unconscious. Probably from the pain and the cold."

"What happened with his hand? What did the doctor say about it?"

Emma's mouth pursed into a thin line. "We don't have a doctor in these parts. Not all the time anyway. There's a surgeon who travels from fort to fort, but he wasn't anywhere close at that time. My aunt is an excellent healer, and Simeon knows a lot about the herbs and plants that are good for curing. The surgeon looked at it when he came a month after the accident but said there wasn't anything he could do."

Those last few statements jogged a memory in Monti's mind, but she had one more question before they left the topic of Joseph. "He said he hasn't been able to feel or use the fingers since the injury. Did the doctor think he would ever regain use of them?"

Emma's face took on a weary sadness. "He said it was unlikely. Joseph took that pretty hard. It's been a rough few months since then, and I haven't seen him smile much. At least, not until yesterday."

Monti didn't meet her look. She was barely managing the flurry of butterflies those words created in her midsection. She'd never be able to hide the kiss from Emma if she met the woman's gaze.

Thankfully, a whistle sounded from outside, and Emma straightened. "Simeon's home." She rose to greet her husband, and Monti kept her focus on her food to give the couple privacy. It didn't stop her from hearing the low murmurs and the sound of a kiss.

"Howdy, Miss Bergeron."

She nearly jumped at Simeon's greeting, then looked up and smiled a response. "Hello."

"Sit down, dear. I'll pour you a bowl of stew." Emma moved to the stove.

"Don't have to ask me twice." Simeon took his place at the head of the table, then looked at her. "Joseph had to leave, but I volunteered to see you back to your cabin."

The words slipped through her, not quite making sense. "Leave? To go where?"

Simeon shrugged. "Not sure exactly. We'd just finished up the last calf, and he packed his things and said he had to leave on business. Asked if I'd make sure you got back all right."

Business? Was he going to town for something? He'd mentioned that he sometimes acted as courier for the folks in the area. Maybe he'd received an urgent request.

She tried not to let her disappointment show. She'd worried about what to say to him, but it seemed he'd taken that concern out of her hands. For now, at least.

CHAPTER 14

Keep her, Lord.
~ Joseph's Journal

hree days later, Monti hadn't heard or seen any sign of Joseph. She shouldn't have expected to, though. At least, that's what she told herself. If he'd gone to deliver a message or pick-up supplies from Fort Hamilton, it could take him days or a week to return.

Patience.

Yet, the churning inside her made it hard to wait patiently. No matter how often she told herself she didn't want romantic attachments, she *did* want to see Joseph again. They'd kissed, for mercy's sake. What did he think about that? Did he regret it?

Her horse stumbled over a rock buried in the snow, pulling Monti back to the present as she and Antoine rode toward Hungry Wolf's camp. A heavy snowfall had come two days before, keeping them close to the cabin until now. And what a relief to finally be out.

"Do you think Hollow Oak's family will let us give her the remedy?" She glanced at Antoine as they rode.

He nodded. "They have been open to the other medicines and foods I bring them. I think her mother will be willing."

They would see soon enough, for the Peigan camp came into sight the next minute.

A few children met them at the edge of the clearing, but not so many as had come the first day. Apparently, she wasn't quite as intriguing as she'd been before.

After handing their horses off to one of the youths to tend them, they carried their supplies directly to the lodge where Hollow Oak had been.

Two men sat in front of the fire, smoking from pipes. Both rose as they approached. The older of the two stepped forward and spoke, making hand motions as he did.

Antoine answered, using the same hand motions mixed with scattered Indian words.

The man spoke again, and during his discourse, motioned to the man behind him.

Antoine turned to her. "This is Fighting Elk, the father of Hollow Oak. And his brother, Thunder Rumbles."

Monti nodded to both men and offered as much of a smile as she could muster in the presence of two intimidating braves.

Both braves were tall and clothed in buckskins. The brother, Thunder Rumbles, nodded back, and seemed to scrutinize her. Not in an improper or hostile way, but it made the fine hairs on her arms rise anyway.

Antoine was following the first man toward the teepee, so Monti hurried after them. She could feel the eyes of Thunder Rumbles on her with each step, and she didn't breathe again until she'd stepped inside and the flap closed behind her.

Hollow Oak sat on a low stack of furs. She held something that looked like a carved doll but smiled and bounced when she saw Monti.

That smile melted a warm puddle in Monti's chest, and she knelt to pull the girl into a quick hug. "I've missed you."

The child held up the figurine. "Hurit." At least the word she spoke sounded something like that.

Monti stroked the indentations carved for the doll's hair. "Pretty." Then she stroked Hollow Oak's hair, pulling the loose strands back from her face. "We brought you medicine to help you feel better."

The girl looked into Monti's eyes. A trusting gaze, and Monti tried to return a reassuring smile, despite the way her heart ached to see the dear little one struggling.

Antoine knelt beside her, holding an open piece of leather on his palm. In the center lay some of the mixture they'd brought. Simeon and Emma had spent almost an hour creating the remedy from all manner of herbs and powders they ground into a paste. Then, Emma had mixed in some other treats that she hoped would make it more palatable for the girl.

Antoine spoke an Indian word, and the girl took the mixture and popped it into her mouth. Emma had said the medicine might be spicy, but Hollow Oak showed no sign of distaste.

"Can I look at your feet?" She pointed to the fur covering the girl's legs.

The girl seemed to acquiesce. When Monti pulled the blanket back, Hollow Oak's bare ankles were hard to see in the darkness. As her eyes adjusted to the dimness, the girls swollen feet and legs glared up at her, twice as big as they should have been. More swollen than the last time she saw them, if memory served.

Monti looked at Antoine, who met her gaze. She didn't have to say how the sight worried her, for the same concern reflected in his eyes.

He rose. "Sit and talk with the child. I'll give the mother instructions to continue the treatment."

After Monti had spent a few sweet minutes snuggling with Hollow Oak and playing with the doll, Antoine motioned for them to leave. Monti pressed a kiss to the girl's hair as she raised up a prayer for healing and protection to their Heavenly Father. Only the Lord could heal this precious one.

When they left the lodge, Thunder Rumbles still stood near the doorway. He spoke a few words to Antoine, then nodded. His eyes landed on her and settled there with a hint of a smile. He had a nice smile with strong features and straight white teeth bright against his tawny skin.

They moved on to other lodges, and Antoine passed out various items from the supplies they'd brought. A trinket here, a pouch of herbs there. She followed him, smiling at the people they met and trying to absorb any Indian words she could. There were similar sounds, but the language was so fluid, it was hard to tell which sounds belonged to what word, much less what the words actually meant.

Antoine had taught her a few of the hand signs that were a common language across many of the tribes, so she could at least decipher those when he resorted to sign language.

After several hours, they prepared to leave. Antoine had just asked the youth to fetch their horses, when Hollow Oak's father strode toward them.

At sight of his determined stride, Monti's heart surged into her throat. Had the girl worsened? Maybe the medicine wasn't sitting well with her. She studied his face, but he didn't seem concerned. He just wore that same stoic look he'd had earlier.

He motioned for Antoine to step to the side with him, which the priest did. The boy came with their horses, and she took both sets of reins. She wasn't about to mount, though, until she knew whether they were needed again. She stroked the velvety nose of first one animal, then the other, as she watched the men talking.

They were using a lot of hand motions, and then Antoine shook his head no. He looked over at her, a bemused look on his face. Then he turned back to the Indian and gestured some more.

At last, Fighting Elk turned and strode back toward his lodge, his regal bearing evident with every step.

Antoine joined her again, and she raised her brows in question. He shook his head and prepared to mount his horse. Curious, but smart enough not to ask again, she mounted hers.

After they rounded the bend that blocked the Indian village from their sight, Monti turned to her cousin. "What did he say?"

Antoine's weathered face seemed to grow even more haggard. His gaze rose to stare off into the distance, but he didn't speak.

She tried to be patient. He wasn't that talkative by nature and often seemed to ponder his words before he spoke them. But it seemed like at least two or three minutes passed, and he still stared ahead.

"Antoine." She worked to keep her tone light and questioning. He'd heard her, she knew. She just had to remind him she would continue waiting until he answered.

The corners of his eyes creased. "You are much like your mother, ma fifille, in so many ways. Not the least of which was her determination." He gave her a sidelong glance from the corner of his eye. "Some might call it stubbornness."

She worked to hold back her smile, but it was a challenge. "Then you're quite aware that I'll not rest until you tell me whatever it is you're not sure I should know."

He glanced at her, then returned his focus to the trail ahead. "Thunder Rumbles has asked for you to be his woman. He is prepared to trade ten horses."

She took in such a sharp breath of biting air, her lungs revolted in a gagging cough. It gave her a second for her thoughts to whirl in twenty directions. His *woman*? Like...marry? She'd only just met the man, and they hadn't even exchanged one word. They didn't speak the same language, for mercy's sake.

When she caught her breath, she turned to look at him. The idea was so ludicrous, she let fly the one spot of humor she could find. "Ten horses. Is that a lot for a woman?"

He chuckled. That deep, rich laugh she'd always loved. "I wouldn't say a lot. If you're keen on the idea, I'll barter for fifty."

She couldn't decide if she should be offended, appalled, or honored. The whole idea was almost more than she could wrap her mind around. She eyed her cousin. "Are you jesting?"

Another chuckle. "Nay, I jest not. He says you have a good and generous heart, and he believes you will make him a good squaw."

"And what did you tell him?"

"At first I said you had just arrived and I would not allow you to marry so soon. Then Fighting Elk insisted I ask your thoughts on the offer. Perhaps you were already taken with Thunder Rumbles. I told him I would discuss it with you."

Monti's jaw dropped. "So you didn't end the matter? They still await an answer?"

He nodded. "Oui."

A long breath seeped out of her as she turned back to the trail. "Well." And that was the only word she could summon.

~

*J*oseph stood at the edge of the mountain, staring out over the backbone of the world, the name the Indians had given the Rockies. These mountains always settled him, but this last week and a half, they'd lost their calming touch.

It would take time to get over Monti. To leave her memory behind. Time and distance.

How could he have fallen for her so thoroughly? Because he'd definitely fallen. With that he'd come to terms during his first day on the trail. He'd never known what it was to love a woman and had never spent much time thinking about what it might feel like.

If this piercing ache in his chest was any kind of sign, he might just love Monticello Bergeron. But he couldn't act on it. Or rather, his action had to be to run far, far away. If he loved her, he would stay out of her life. She deserved someone so much better than him—a crippled vagabond.

Which begged the question, why hadn't he traveled farther? He'd not moved more than half a day's ride from the priest's cabin for a week and a half now. He might not be visiting the woman, but couldn't seem to put the distance between them that would let the ache in his chest start to heal.

If only he weren't crippled. But even then, would he really be worthy of Monti? She was beautiful and strong and intelligent. And he was...a vagrant. A wanderer. With nothing to recommend him.

Turning away from the cliff's edge, he mounted Copper, then pointed the horse down the mountain trail.

~

"Today, we return to Hungry Wolf's camp."

Monti straightened from stirring the porridge and faced her cousin. "I think it might be best for you to go settle things and I'll stay here today."

They hadn't discussed the marriage proposal in the week since it had been offered, but she'd spent more than one restless night turning the whole scenario over and over in her mind. It wasn't that she was opposed to marrying an Indian. She'd heard many white trappers took Indian wives, so how much different would this be?

It was all the other things that separated them. Language. The fact she'd barely met the man. She had no idea if he was decent or violent or a drunkard. But the strongest of all barriers between them was the fact that, as far as she knew, none of the Indians in that camp had turned from their worship of the sun to discover the one true God. Perhaps Antoine would be honest and give that as the reason for her refusal. Surely the Indians would understand, and would see how important God was in their lives. Maybe it would spur some of the natives to learn more about Him.

If Thunder Rumbles did find faith in God, could she accept his suit then? She could barely stomach the thought. Mostly because her heart ached so much over Joseph's absence. Where had he gone? She and Antoine even visited Emma a few days before, but they'd not seen or heard from him since the last time she had.

Her heart told her he was staying away on purpose. Her mind occasionally tried to argue the point, saying he likely had legitimate reasons for not returning yet. But as surely as she knew she'd come to love the man, she also knew he was avoiding her. And the pain that thought brought on was almost too much to face.

Which made it even harder to deal with the idea of an Indian suitor. Any suitor, other than Joseph.

Antoine's hand rested on her shoulder, and she turned to face him. "It is best for us both to go. You know it, too. I will explain that our faith does not allow you to be unequally yoked with an unbeliever, but you must show you have no malice toward the man. Show him the heart of Jesus." He cupped his hands over the spot where his own heart resided.

She couldn't help but smile at this wise man who'd been such a strong influence in her life, even from hundreds of miles away. "If I must."

CHAPTER 15

The turmoil swirls both within and without. Set my mind on You, Father.
Press Your seal upon my wayward heart.
~ Monti's Journal

*A*s Monti neared the Indian camp with the priest, the knot in her middle twisted tighter. What if Thunder Rumbles grew angry at her refusal? Would he be violent? She knew so little about these people and their customs. Her response would likely be a great insult to him.

She glanced over at Antoine. Should she ask him about it? If Joseph were here, this knot of fear would untangle. She never felt anything but protected by his side.

But, no. She couldn't discuss another man's marriage offer with Joseph. Not when she longed for the proposal to be from him. She jerked her back straight. Where had that thought come from? She was married to her Lord now. She had no need for a man.

When they entered the camp, the place seemed quieter than

normal. At the lodge where Hollow Oak's family lived, no men sat around the fire as they had before. The woman met them at the door flap and motioned them inside.

Monti's chest squeezed as she saw the empty pallet where the girl usually lay. Then a movement from the side caught her attention.

"Monti." The girl cried her name as she launched herself into Monti's arms.

Monti held her close, breathing in the sweetness of the pudgy arms around her. "How are you? Has the medicine helped you feel better?"

Hollow Oak chattered in her little-girl voice, and Monti dropped to her knees to watch the girl's expression as she spoke. It was impossible to understand a single word, but the animation on her face proved how much better she seemed to be feeling than she had the last two times they'd visited.

At last, Monti turned to Antoine and the young squaw. "How has she been?"

Antoine spoke up. "Her mother says she has taken the tonic steadily and has seemed better, little by little. She's been up and playing with the others for three or four days now."

The good news eased the tension in her chest, but only a little. "Too much activity may not be good. She should take lots of rests."

He nodded and began signing to the woman.

Monti turned back to the girl, who grabbed her hand and spoke again as she pulled Monti outside.

A commotion seemed to be coming from the outskirts of camp, and Hollow Oak dragged her to a spot where they could see between the teepees. A group of Indians rode at a fast clip over the hill, slowing their horses as they reached the lodges.

People came pouring from the teepees and clamored around the riders who paraded through camp. Hollow Oak pulled her forward to join the group, although she wasn't altogether sure she wanted to be caught up in the throng. Still, she couldn't help but be curious.

The riders were all men, all tall and regal on their horses. A war party, perhaps? She didn't see any paint on their faces or the horses like she'd heard they applied before battle. A few men pulled extra horses with large packs over their backs. Maybe they'd just returned from a long journey. That would explain the enthusiastic greeting.

Then she saw the deer draped across the back of one of the horses. Some of the other packs began to take solid forms as she studied them differently. Perhaps this was a hunting party then?

She scanned the men's face, and her breath caught when she recognized one. Thunder Rumbles. About fifty paces away, his gaze locked on her as the group moved her direction. Even from this distance, she could see the way a smile played at the corners of his mouth.

She wanted to shrink back, to spin around and hide behind a lodge. Or better yet, run back to their horses and ride home. But instead, she offered a kind nod and moved her gaze away from him.

There were a dozen or more riders, maybe closer to twenty. Another figure near the rear of the group caught her attention. It couldn't be who she'd thought at first glance. Her mind had so latched onto her heart's longing for Joseph, she was seeing him everywhere now. The figure wore a fur skin coat like the other men's, although it seemed fashioned more like a white man's coat than the loose robes the Indians wore.

It was probably the copper colored horse he rode that made her see Joseph in the man. And that special set to his shoulders she'd studied for day after day on their journey from Fort Hamilton.

As the Indians moved nearer, the lead horses began to pass her. Yet she couldn't take her gaze from the man in the back of the group.

People thronged around her, and Antoine's voice sounded just behind her. He spoke in French, the words roughly translating to "I cannot believe my eyes."

She spun to look at him. Did he think it was Joseph, too? Or did his comment refer to something else entirely?

Antoine's gaze dropped to hers with an absent-minded smile, then raised back up to the Indians. Or rather, to the man in the back who looked like Joseph.

He was within twenty strides of her now, his posture relaxed as he scanned the crowd, somewhat bemused by the excitement. She'd seen that look on Joseph's face before. It had to be him.

Then his gaze landed on her, locking with hers. The shock that swept over his face lasted only a moment, then slipped behind a mask as he pulled his focus from her and pointed it at the horse in front of him.

She kept her focus on him as he passed by and until several horses and riders separated them. Soon, the riders disbursed as the throng swallowed them up.

Monti turned to Antoine, who gave her a knowing look. "We must talk to Fighting Elk and his brother. Then we will seek out our friend."

She nodded. *Give me strength, Lord.*

When they reached Fighting Elk's lodge, the young squaw stood outside gesturing to the two men with one hand while she held the ropes of their two horses with her other. The animals dozed behind her, loaded with bundles wrapped in animal skins. All three people seemed to see Antoine and her at the same time and ceased talking as they approached.

The squaw walked toward them, leading the horses behind her. She came near Monti and touched her arm, then motioned for Monti to accompany her.

What now? Monti glanced at Antoine, who nodded.

"Go with her. I think she wants to give me a private moment to discuss matters with the men."

The woman motioned again, and Monti forced herself to turn and follow. They walked in silence toward the edge of the camp where a cluster of horses stood. When they neared the other animals, the woman handed one of the ropes to Monti, then started to unfasten the leather bindings holding the furs on her horse's back.

She motioned toward the animal Monti held, apparently wanting her to do the same. Within a few minutes, they had both horses turned loose with the others and were carrying the packs back toward the lodge. It might have been easier to remove these when the horses had been standing by the teepee, except that the squaw had been in such a hurry to get her away.

As they walked, Monti pointed toward herself and spoke her name. The woman jabbed at her own chest and spoke a string of syllables that sounded something like "Dashanashi."

Monti tried to repeat the sounds back to her, but she must have butchered the word.

The Indian woman smiled, then pointed at herself again and said, "Dashi."

"Dashi." Monti repeated the shortened version. Much easier to pronounce.

The squaw smiled again, then nodded. Apparently, that was close enough.

As they neared Dashi's lodge, Monti forced herself not to drop back. The braves still stood outside and seemed to be talking to Antoine with hand signals.

Dashi motioned for Monti to place her load at the edge of their camp, which she did.

Antoine motioned her over. "I have told them of the importance of shared faith between man and wife. Thunder Rumbles understands, as his beliefs are important to him, as well."

A weight seemed to slip off her shoulders, and she glanced at the man in question. He eyed Antoine, as though trying to make out his words. Not once did his gaze slip to her.

Antoine touched her arm and leaned closer as his voice softened. "They have invited me to smoke the pipe and tell of our faith. Why don't you find Monsieur Malcom while I share with these men?"

She nodded, trying to keep her expression passive. Not an easy feat with her emotions swirling like a windstorm.

$\approx$

*J*oseph stood talking to Three Shadows, the brave who'd invited him to join their hunt. It had seemed like a good way to get his mind off Monti. The last thing he'd expected was to run into her here in the camp.

He should mount his horse and ride off now before she approached him. Except that would be the coward's way of handling this situation. He did enough things he hated. He didn't need to add being a coward to the list.

There. Monti appeared around the corner of a lodge, every inch the French princess she'd always been. She saw him then, her chin notching up as she marched straight toward him. So brave and pretty and headstrong.

She stopped in front of him, and he had to fight the urge to step forward and pull her closer. Press his mouth to hers and taste the sweetness he'd dreamed about for a week and a half. A breeze blew the loose tendrils of her hair across her face, adding to the stubborn independence plainly showing there.

He had to be the one to speak first. He knew that. He'd left without a farewell, an insult that was his to make right. He swallowed to summon moisture back into his mouth. "Hello." A great orator, he was not.

"Hello." Her voice wasn't harsh but lacked its usually softness. "I didn't expect to see you here."

"I saw Three Shadows in the mountains." He motioned toward his friend, but the man had walked away. Probably to give them privacy. "He invited me on the hunt. What brings you to this village?"

She raised her brows. "We were checking on Hollow Oak and had some other business."

It might have been the cold, but her face seemed to color with her words. "How is she? Do you still think it's a heart condition?"

She nodded. "Simeon sent a concoction of herbals that seem to have helped some. At least she's up and moving now."

He frowned. "She's been abed all this time?" That would be unusual for any youngster, especially a hardy Indian child.

"For almost a week I think."

His chest squeezed at the thought of the little one in pain. "What else can be done for her?"

Lines formed across her brow. "We're doing everything I know, and she seems to be progressing. I hope it's enough. I pray it's enough."

Silence settled between them, and he struggled for something to say. There was so much, but everything he thought of brought his mind back to their kiss.

At last, he asked, "Where's the priest?"

She glanced behind her, as though checking to see. Then she turned back to him. "He's speaking with Thunder Rumbles...and Fighting Elk." She didn't meet his eye. "They have asked...about his faith."

Something wasn't right there. The way she wouldn't meet his gaze, her hands clasping tightly around themselves. And more color seemed to have flooded her face than could be attributed to the cold. His gut told him to dig deeper.

"Fighting Elk is the father of Hollow Oak?" He waited her response.

She nodded.

"And Thunder Rumbles is...?"

She glanced behind her again. Was it so he couldn't see her face? "He's the brother of Fighting Elk."

"Do you know these men?"

"I've only met them a couple of times."

"It's a wonder they've agreed to hear Father Bergeron. What happened to encourage them?"

She did meet his gaze then, raising her chin in a stubborn jut. Something about the look in her eyes made his gut tighten. "Thunder Rumbles asked for my hand in marriage. Antoine let him know our faith discourages yoking with an unbeliever, so he asked for details of our beliefs."

Even though he'd prepared for a blow, her words slammed into him, shaking him all the way to his core. So many thoughts churned in his mind, but he forced his voice to remain calm. "You aren't considering marrying him if he converts?" Perhaps his tone was too calm. Almost lethal in its lack of emotion.

She still held his gaze, but her eyes softened a touch. "I hadn't planned to marry anyone."

He couldn't begin to explain the relief her words brought on. Yet, not completely.

A commotion sounded behind him. Someone yelling, a child screaming.

He whirled, trying to decipher the Indian words. Children were running from the trees, waving and calling frantically. When he caught the word *dead*, his instincts came alive.

Sprinting toward the children, he signed for them to tell him what was wrong.

The youths crowded around him and pulled at his arms, but couldn't seem to calm enough to answer him.

One of the older children motioned him to follow and said something that sounded like Hollow Oak's Indian name. A pit of dread filled his stomach, and he glanced backward to see where Monti was.

Right behind him.

She'd grown especially attached to the child. If something had happened to Hollow Oak—if she'd died—the last thing he wanted was Monti with him when he found the scene.

He motioned her back. "Stay here. I'll go see what's wrong."

She shook her head. "I'll come too. Maybe I can help."

Other Indians were running from the village now, and every moment might mean the difference for the child.

He turned back to the youth. "Show me."

They ran through the snow, into the forest of lodgepole pine and cedar. The other children straggled behind, but the youth he followed ran like a mountain lion. Long strides stretching as he wove through the trees.

At last, they reached a narrow river. The surface had frozen over except for a small hole at the bank where the ice was broken.

A hole just the size of a little girl.

He slid down the steep part of the embankment, then dropped to his knees on the jut of land at the edge of the water and peered in. The ice was three or four inches thick, and the water underneath looked dark from the shadows, but relatively clear.

No sign of a person.

He turned back to the youth, pointing into the water. "Hollow Oak is in there?"

The lad shook his head and motioned down the river a little, where the steep embankment met the water. The river's flow had eaten away at the lower part of the earth, making a sort of ledge under which a small figure now lay slumped on the ice.

Monti saw her first and rushed to the place where the jut of land ended, still four or five feet from the girl. They would have to crawl out on the ice to reach her.

"Don't, Monti." He made it to her and grabbed her waist so she didn't do something foolish. "The ice won't hold you."

"I have to get to her. She's passed out. If we don't do something to fix her heart, she'll die." She struck at him, landing a hard blow in his chest. Harder than he'd expected, and it punched the breath out of him.

She took advantage of that slight distraction to squirm free from his arms. She dropped to her knees and scooted onto the ice.

"Monti." He sank to his own hands and knees, then grabbed her skirt, barely registering the familiar brown wool he'd bought at the Fort Hamilton trading post all those weeks ago. "Come back."

She reached the girl and gathered her into her arms. The child's head hung backward as Monti cradled her, all her limbs falling limp.

He eyed the ice, but no cracks seemed to be working out from beneath her. Of course, he knew from experience the ice could suddenly give way without any previous sign of weakness. He'd almost lost his sister from a sudden fall through the ice, and the memories created a swirl of panic in his chest. "Monti, please. Ease your way back now."

She did as he asked, and he didn't breathe until she and the child inched onto solid ground.

He helped her settle Hollow Oak in her arms. The girl still lay unconscious, and her body was cold, so cold. The bile churning in his gut rose up into his throat.

She couldn't be... Surely she was not dead.

CHAPTER 16

Though my mind knows better, my heart still reaches.
~ Joseph's Journal

Monti held the girl close and pressed two fingers to the artery at her neck. It was there. A faint pulse.

She looked up into Joseph's face. "She lives. But we have to get her back to camp. Have to get her warm and see what else is wrong."

He reached out. "Let me carry her."

She didn't hesitate to put the girl in his arms. He could be trusted to take the utmost care of her.

He cradled Hollow Oak, resting her head in the crook of his arm so it didn't bounce. His injured hand didn't seem to get in his way at all.

They rose and turned toward the embankment, which would be work for him to climb with a load in his arms.

Worried Indians gathered at the top, both young and grown. Monti climbed behind Joseph as he strode up the steep side, and she

130

kept a hand at his back in case he lost his balance. His footing was sure, though.

Dashi came running through the throng of people, sobbing as she approached Joseph and the child. She pressed a hand to her mouth, her eyes welling.

Monti squeezed her shoulder. "She lives. She's alive still."

Dashi looked at her, her dark eyes glistening as she seemed to be trying to understand.

Joseph had already started back toward the camp. Monti took the woman's arm, and they ran in his wake.

Dashi was practically dragging her as they reached the lodge, for Monti could scarce catch her breath.

Inside, Joseph was kneeling over Hollow Oak's pallet, Antoine at his side. The two Indian men hovered a few feet behind.

The young squaw gave a little cry as she took in the scene, then rushed forward and dropped to her knees by her daughter's head.

Hollow Oak was awake, thank the Lord. Monti joined the group, and Joseph shifted backward to give her his position.

"We need to get her warm." His words were a comforting breath at her ear.

She nodded and pulled the animal-skin robes up tighter around the girl. Dashi seemed to get the idea, and worked to snuggle her daughter tighter in the furs.

"The medicine." Monti twisted to look around the lodge. "She needs to take some. It'll help her blood flow."

"I'll get it." Antoine groaned as he pushed to his feet.

Monti turned back to focus on the girl again.

Her normally dark lips had lightened to an eerie blueish tint. Her teeth chattered, but as her eyes met Monti, she tried to smile. "M-m-monti."

The smile started a fresh wave of panic in Monti's chest. The left side of her face didn't move. That part of her mouth didn't pull up. That adorable girlish grin that had stolen Monti's heart from their first meeting only formed on the right side.

What do I do, Lord? She'd read about this type of apoplexy, but mostly in older people. It was thought to be caused by injury to the brain. Could it have something to do with her heart condition? Or perhaps it happened with the fall on the ice.

If the former, she could only pray the tonic helped. If the latter, rest might be the best medicine for the girl.

Hollow Oak took the mixture willingly. She was such an obliging child, even during trauma and illness. When she'd finished a double dose, Dashi cradled the girl in her arms, rocking gently and murmuring.

"She needs much rest. Can you tell her that?" Monti looked to her cousin.

He nodded and made several hand gestures to the mother. Dashi responded with a nod, then snuggled her daughter closer. Hollow Oak's eyes drifted shut, which made her face look normal again.

It didn't stop Monti's own heart from aching in her chest, though. Why had something like this had to happen to such a sweet, innocent little girl?

$\sim$

*A*s Joseph followed the priest and Monti out of the lodge, he nodded to Hollow Oak's father, who stood by the fire outside. He looked grim, more than the normal stoic expression the Indian men often wore. The man beside him must be his brother.

Joseph couldn't help but stiffen as he walked past. He must be the one who'd offered for Monti. What had she called him? Thunder Rumbles?

He nodded at the man, whose eyes narrowed as he studied Joseph.

Father Bergeron approached the men and spoke with them for a moment, leaving Joseph standing with Monti on the outskirts of the fire's warmth. He wanted to talk to her, to ask how she'd been. To hear her musical voice again. To erase the worry that lined her face. Which might require wrapping her in his arms. Holding her tight and inhaling her softness.

But when he glanced at her, she was looking at Thunder Rumbles.

A knife of jealousy stabbed his gut. But maybe it was better this way, if the man was willing to consider Christianity. If he valued Monti enough to change his faith for her, perhaps he would be the husband she deserved.

If only things could be as simple for Joseph. If all he needed to be worthy of this woman was to make peace with God, he'd put forth the effort.

God may have lost track of him in this mountain wilderness, but maybe the Almighty would hear for Monti's sake. Yet that wouldn't make his hand work again. That wouldn't make him the man he wished he could be. Would it?

"Let us journey home now." The priest clamped a hand on Joseph's shoulder. "Come with us, Joseph. We've missed you these past days."

One look at the kind eyes and wisdom-lined face had him nodding. "Yes, sir. I can ride along."

Within a quarter hour, they were out of camp and riding over the hill toward the priest's cabin. The trail was wide enough for two to ride abreast, but not three. He found himself riding beside Monti, the priest just ahead.

The older man made small talk about his conversations with the Indians, speaking mostly to Monti. Joseph kept an ear tuned for mention of Thunder Rumbles, but most of his focus strained toward the woman riding tall in the saddle beside him, although he rarely let himself look her direction.

"Did my young cousin tell you we've been to visit the Blood tribe in Greenriver Gap?" This the priest directed toward him. "I was most pleased with their response to her. Very encouraging."

Joseph glanced sharply at Monti. "Isn't that the group you said has been ill? Isn't there danger of contagion still?"

Monti shook her head, her chin jutting. "There's some form of danger in everything. If the potential for good outweighs the risk, I'll not stand back and wait."

She was too feisty for her own good. But that was part of what made her such an enigma. Delicate and cultured one moment, striding right through the bounds of decorum the next if she saw a need she could fill.

"We saw a huge herd of buffalo on that trip." Her determination softened some, and she offered a tentative smile. "You should have seen them. They covered the land so the ground looked black. I'd have never thought it possible."

"It is a sight to behold, isn't it?" Joseph said. "I saw my first herd when we were on the steamboat bound for the Montana Territory. I'll never forget the way they blanketed the plains beside the Missouri River. And sometimes they'd walk right out into the water, and the boat would have to wait hours for the herd to cross."

The rest of the trip seemed shorter than normal, but when they reined in at the lean-to behind the cabin, the dusky light that comes before sunset had fallen over the land. He'd not eaten since breakfast, and his stomach was gnawing on his backbone. Which made it hard to say no when the priest invited him in for the evening meal.

"Food sounds good. Much obliged." He glanced at Monti, who was loosening the saddle from her mare. Had she made any progress with her cooking skills during the time he'd stayed away? "I can settle your horse if you need to get inside."

"I'm almost done. And I already have food cooked, just need to warm it." She grabbed the heavy leather contraption and hoisted it off the animal.

Leaving his own horse standing, he strode to her and grabbed her saddle with his good hand. She let him take it, which was a good thing, since it probably weighed almost as much as she did. Or at least half as much.

She'd released her mount in the corral and headed inside before he and Father Bergeron finished with their own horses.

He fell into step beside the man on their way toward the front door. "I hope me staying isn't an imposition."

"Non. We are always pleased when you visit. My cousin is..." The priest seemed to choose his words carefully. "She has much that is new to her since coming to this land. New people. New work. Her heart is conflicted about some of the changes, but she will sort through them. I have no doubt."

Her heart is conflicted. About him? Or about the Indian who wanted to marry her?

They reached the door and stepped inside. The rich aroma of beans met his senses, and Monti scurried from the hearth to the table and back again.

"Wash up for the meal, then take your seats." She motioned toward a bucket of water sitting against one wall. That certainly hadn't been there the last time he'd visited, and he had to bite back a smile as he followed the priest and waited his turn with the water. A woman's touch was usually a good thing.

The food was excellent, and he took the first opportunity to tell her so.

"Merci." Her face seemed to pink as she smiled down into her bowl of beans. "I can manage a few meals now without burning them." When she glanced up, a twinkle shone in her dark eyes.

"And where do you go from here, my friend?" Father Bergeron used a flapjack to sop beans from his dish.

"I need to stop in at my sister's. If I don't check in with them every couple of weeks, Emma tends to get ornery."

"That will require much travel tonight after dark. Stay the night here and leave out in the morning." He glanced at his niece. "Monti will ride with you. She was just saying yesterday she would like to visit your good family again."

A cough spewed from Monti, and she clapped a hand to her mouth, probably to keep the food from spilling out. Her face reddened, and she looked to be struggling to speak.

The sight was so charming, it made his response come out before he thought through it. "If I wouldn't be in the way, I'd be happy to wait and escort Miss Monti to visit my family."

Monti finally swallowed whatever was clogging her throat and gasped a loud breath. "I have far too much to do for a visit tomorrow. But thanks for the offer."

Her refusal sent a pang to his chest, tightening his muscles. "Monti." He spoke low, and waited for her to look at him.

It took her a moment, as she busied herself by pushing beans around in her bowl with her spoon. Finally, she raised her gaze to meet his. There was a defiant spark there that pressed harder on his lungs. She'd not have this wariness now if he hadn't hurt her. The last thing he wanted was for her to suffer on his account.

"Monti, I'd be honored if you'd ride with me to Emma's place. You need a visit, and so does she. I'll make myself scarce when we get there, if that'll help any."

The spark eased, but only a little, and the hint of pain she seemed to be trying to mask made him feel lower than a mangy dog in a back alley.

"All right." She dropped her gaze back to her bowl.

How had he made such a mess of things? Did her anger stem from his having left right after their kiss? He'd done it to save her from himself. But maybe she didn't understand exactly why she would be better off without him.

His mind dropped instantly to the crippled fingers on his left hand. She'd seen his hand without the glove, but maybe she didn't realize exactly what it meant.

He slid a sideways glance at her. Her head was down. Not the Monti he'd fallen in love with. And the last thing he wanted was to take away her joy. If it required him to reveal his defects to prove she'd not lost anything worth keeping, so be it.

CHAPTER 17

At last, the chance to set the record straight.
~ Monti's Journal

Lord, I don't want to be angry with him. Monti scrubbed the last of the food remnants from the bean pot, then poured in a bit of clean water to slosh around. Joseph's presence had her spirit so agitated, she'd been unfit company by the time they sat down to eat.

She had to get control over herself. *Take this anger, Father. Show me how to help him.*

The door opened behind her, but she didn't turn to look. She'd know soon enough by the boot thuds which of the men had returned from settling the animals.

The tread was somewhat light, not heavy and determined. It must be Antoine coming in to warm his tired bones. He'd settle in his chair by the fire, don his spectacles, and open his Bible or a book of sermons.

She pushed to her feet and reached for one of the cups she'd just cleaned, then the teapot she'd kept steeping to warm him after being outside. After filling the mug, she replaced the pot and turned toward Antoine.

But it wasn't him.

Joseph stood a few feet inside the doorway, watching her. He'd removed his coat and hat but still wore his gloves. The gloves he never took off.

She didn't let her gaze linger on them but focused on his face and tried to summon a welcoming smile. Even if she didn't feel welcoming, maybe her actions would eventually bring her emotions into line.

She took a step forward and extended the mug to him. "This will warm you. I'm sure it's cold outside."

He took the cup, but his gaze never left her face. His mouth parted as though he wanted to say something, but he didn't speak. Then his focus dropped to the mug, and a breath later, he rested it on the table.

Her gaze followed his movement, steeling herself for whatever he was about to say. Maybe he planned to explain his absence for the last week and a half. The reason he'd left so suddenly after their kiss. Maybe the reason he'd kissed her at all, if he felt nothing for her.

Raising his face, he leveled his gaze on her. "Monti. There's something I need to tell you."

This was it. She nodded, preparing her face and body not to react to whatever he said.

He pulled the leather glove from his right hand, and she couldn't help but drop her gaze to the action. He moved so deliberately, as though this was part of his explanation.

When he laid that glove on the table and reached for the left hand, everything clicked into place in her mind. *His injury was part of the explanation.*

Her gaze flew to his face, searching for trepidation.

It was there aplenty. But determination seemed to drive him on.

As much as she wanted to see his hand again, she wanted to prove to him that his injury didn't define him. He didn't have to hide it like the lepers hid their sores back in Biblical days.

His Adam's apple bobbed.

She kept her focus on his face. But at the edges of her vision, she could just see that his glove was off, yet she couldn't make out any detail.

"Look at my hand, Monti." Joseph's voice was tight, almost angry.

She swallowed, searching his hard eyes. "Why?"

He took a step forward. The hand became slightly clearer as he raised it, extended it toward her.

She didn't look, just kept her gaze locked on his.

"I want you to see what's wrong with me. See why I'm no good for you. I'm a cripple. I'll never be who you need." He growled the words.

He wanted his statement to make her feel differently—that was plain from the almost belligerent look on his face. And they did. Those words broke through the barrier she'd built around her emotions, pushing her into action.

Without lowering her gaze from his, she stepped forward, closing the distance between them. Shock tinged his eyes for a moment, then they narrowed as he watched her. As though he was trying to protect himself. Maintain the armor shrouding his heart.

They were through with armor.

She reached her right hand for his left, lifting it upward so their palms touched. She wove her fingers through his, never taking her focus from his face.

With their hands intertwined, she held their joined hands up between them, stroking with her thumb. "I've seen your hand." *Give me the words, Lord.* "I knew it bothered you, but I still can't fathom why you believe it has any bearing on your worth."

She pressed her free hand to his chest. "You are the man God made you to be, Joseph Malcom. The things that happened to you don't have the power to make you more or less than that. It's up to you to decide whether you'll live up to His plan for you."

She waited then, sending up another prayer that Joseph would accept her words. Or at least not reject them outright. His face showed a struggle that made her chest ache. *Should I say something else, Lord?* Something that would help her declarations find fertile soil?

The Lord didn't seem to be pressing any words of wisdom on her heart, so she held her tongue. And her breath.

At last, Joseph let out a long sigh. His shoulders sagged. "I know you saw it that night. In Emma's barn. But had you seen it before? That night I fell asleep with the guitar?" His eyes had weary lines at the edges.

"Yes. I wanted to ask you what happened after that, but from the way you kept it covered, I thought it might be best to wait until you brought it up." The niggle in her gut that had started a minute before now grew more insistent. She had to tell all. If he found out from his sister…

She cleared the lump in her throat. "I, um, asked your sister about the scar."

He winced, then opened his eyes and scrutinized her. "I would have expected Emma to keep my secrets, but something tells me she didn't. Did she?"

Monti pursed her lips against a smile. "No. She was more forthcoming than I expected. She's worried about you." She pulled their joined hands closer and pressed a kiss to one of his cold knuckles.

He cringed and tried to pull his hand away from her. "I hate the sight of it."

She looked down at the hand, finally, letting him see her scrutinize it. She tipped her head to see the crimson scar, then craned her neck the other way to see the way his fingers curved limply over her hand. She pulled her fingers from his, flattening her hand so his lay level across hers, fingers to palm.

Then she took his other hand and did the same with her left hand. Now she held both of his flat hands in hers. Without flicking a glance at his face, she examined the backs of both his hands, moving her head back and forth so he would see that she looked at everything. The similarities. The differences.

After another breath, she looked up at him, taking in every line of his face. The depth of uncertainty in his amber eyes. The vulnerability. Did he really worry she thought less of him because of an injury?

But it was there, written on his face, sculpted in his gaze. It made her chest pull tight. Emotion sting the backs of her eyes.

She spread his arms wide and stepped into them, pulling them around behind her so his hands rested on her back. Then she pressed her hands to his chest and met his gaze, pouring every ounce of certainty she possessed into her words. "You are perfect, Joseph Malcom. You only need be the man God made you to be. That's enough for me."

His throat worked. He inhaled an audible breath, then released it. The tension and angst seemed to leave his shoulders with the exhale.

Then his gaze drifted down to her mouth, and she knew what was coming.

~

*T*he next morning, the lightness in Monti's chest wouldn't let her keep from smiling. Especially when she succeeded in broiling the hare, an early morning gift from Joseph, without burning it or the Johnny cakes. She was getting the hang of this cooking. Hopefully Emma would show her some new recipes today, too.

Antoine seemed amused by her cheerful demeanor, and from the way he watched her, it appeared he had a good idea what caused it. What did he think about Joseph? They'd discussed how he seemed to have a burden about him, and Antoine said he hadn't noticed that the first few times he'd met the man. Which made sense, given the accident.

If Joseph now realized that the loss of his hand didn't make people think any less of him, perhaps the weight that burdened him would be lifted. *Free him, Father.*

As it had so many times through the night and that morning, the kiss from the evening before filtered into her thoughts while she readied for the trip to Emma's. Joseph had seemed tentative at first, but then his kiss had turned almost…hungry. She'd not been much better. Just the memory of her response sent a wave of embarrassment flaming through her.

A sound drifted through the blanket that shielded her sleeping quarters from the rest of the cabin. The door opening, then closing.

"Are you ready, cousin? Joseph has the horses waiting in front."

She pulled the hood of her coat up to cover her head and neck, then grabbed the saddle bags she'd packed with a few provisions and ducked around the blanket. "All set."

When she stepped outside, the morning sky hadn't brightened much from when she'd gone out right after dawn to gather fresh snow for cooking. Gray clouds hung low in the sky, portending another bout of weather. Most likely snow.

Joseph stood with the horses, both sets of reins in his right hand, his left tucked in a pocket.

She couldn't help but smile at the rugged sight of him in his furskin coat. He met her gaze, and the corner of his mouth tipped in that roguish half-smile. The one that lit a fire all the way down to her toes.

Thank heaven for Antoine's tread behind her, or she'd get caught up in the sight before her. She turned to her cousin. "Are you sure you won't join us? I know Emma and her family would love to see you."

He patted her shoulder. "I considered it, but my spirit urges me to spend quiet time with the Lord. I'll be better for it when you return."

Quiet time with the Lord. Other than her steady stream of thank you's and requests, she'd not sat still with her Bible and prayer journal that morning, nor silenced her mind and heart to hear His words and direction. *I'm sorry, Father.*

She squeezed Antoine's hand. "I'll see you before dark comes."

As she and Joseph rode through the morning chill, the old familiar camaraderie returned. She asked about all he'd been doing while he was gone, and he told of his cave again and the day trips he'd made into the surrounding areas.

He asked about her visit to the tribe of Blood Indians, and she filled a good half hour with stories from that particular adventure. It seemed like every undertaking was an adventure in this land, even this simple trip to visit neighbors. What new stories would she have to tell when she returned to Antoine's little cabin tonight?

Snowflakes started falling just before they reached the valley where Joseph's family lived, and the horses seemed to hasten when Emma's cabin came into sight. Did both animals remember this as home?

Joseph reined his horse when they reached the house, then dismounted. "Go on in. I'll put these two away."

As cold as she was, it didn't seem fair to leave him with all the work. She turned her mare toward the barn. "I can help. We'll get it done twice as fast."

"Monti." His voice held a slight edge of warning. Or maybe that was exasperation. "Let a man do his job for once. I'm not completely helpless."

Her heart hitched as the words sank through her. She halted her horse, then slipped down to the ground. It took only a few seconds for her numb feet to support her again, and she turned and marched toward Joseph, stopping in front of him. "I know. I just—" She threw up a hand. "I have so much to learn. The more I do for myself, the more I learn. It's become a habit to participate in everything, I suppose."

She held the reins out to him. "If you want the job, you can have it."

He took them, eyeing her with a twinkle in his amber gaze and a tilt of his mouth.

She couldn't help herself. She reached out and patted the thick layer of coat covering his chest.

He returned the favor by tapping a gloved hand on her chin. For a second, his gaze hovered on her mouth, and her breath caught as she imagined him leaning forward and kissing her. But then his focus moved up to her eyes, and his smile pulled higher.

Later, it seemed to say. *Later*.

CHAPTER 18

This feels better than I deserve. Should I simply accept it?
~ Joseph's Journal

*S*he could spend a lot of happy days like this.

Monti sat on the floor by the hearth in the Grants' main room, little Hannah snuggled in her lap, and the dog, Mustang, stretched out beside her skirts.

"Again." Hannah bounced in her lap and clapped as Simeon strummed the final chord of a feisty Irish ballad. Emma had sung with him, and the pair made a breathtaking duo.

Simeon grinned at his daughter and did a fast strum of the final chord progression again.

She giggled, tucking her chin into her chest.

He sprawled out in his chair as if exhausted. "That's all for me."

"Again." Hannah bounced, her voice more insistent this time.

Simeon passed the guitar to his wife. "Ask Mama. I'm too tired."

"Oh, no, you don't." Emma took the guitar and handed it down to

Joseph, who sat on the floor opposite Monti. "I can't play a tune on this thing to save my soul. Uncle Joey will have to do it."

Monti's breath hitched as she watched him.

He took the instrument his sister thrust into his arms, but then stared at it. The longing in his eyes was plain, but more than just that emotion stirred in the amber depths. Fear?

"Again," Hannah gurgled, clapping her hands.

Joseph looked as though he needed someone to help him believe he could do it. Did she dare?

Wrapping her arms around the child, she leaned close to tuck her cheek against the soft curls. "Did I tell you your Uncle Joey was helping me learn to play the guitar?"

Hannah turned to look at her. "Guitar?"

It was hard not to smile at that little girl face. "Yes. I can play part of it, but he had to play the other part for me. Should we do that again, do you think?"

"Again." The child wiggled this time instead of bouncing.

Monti looked at Joseph and met his gaze. A bit wary, but not resistant. She raised her brows. "Again?"

His chin bobbed less than an inch, but the softening of his face was her real answer.

"All right, Miss Hannah." She picked the child up and set her on her feet. "You go sit with your Mama while your Uncle Joey and I play a song for you."

Monti crawled as gracefully as she could into position on Joseph's left side and took the guitar into her arms.

He removed the glove from his right hand and tucked himself against her side so he could reach the guitar to strum. The warm security of being snuggled next to him was enough to make her wish the song would last all afternoon.

"What shall we play?" His deep vibrato rumbled in her ear, and his breath fanned her neck.

She glanced back at him, but that put their faces only inches apart. Far too intimate for an audience. So she busied herself adjusting her fingers on the frets. "We could play The Green Willow Tree again. I think I've forgotten the chording, though."

He nodded and sent a glance to his sister. "You remember this one, Em." Then he focused on the guitar, leaning over the body. "It starts with an E7 chord." He talked her through the chord progression a couple times, then started a rhythmic strum.

The first time through the chords was a bit ungainly, but she'd fallen into the cadence by the second time. Joseph's low tenor struck into the first verse, and she had the courage to join him on the next line. It wasn't easy playing and singing at the same time.

Emma's sweet soprano joined in on the second verse, and they had a lively chorus going. Hannah bounced and clapped with the music, and Simeon helped her with a little dance in his lap.

The warmth and joy cloaking the group settled over Monti, and she breathed it in as a sweet aroma.

When Joseph strummed the final chord with a prolonged flair, she leaned back into his shoulder and smiled at the group.

Emma clapped. "I love it. Just like old times." Her gaze found Joseph's, and a special smile crept over her face. Full of memories and thoughts that only siblings—or maybe just twins—could communicate with a look. Monti had never had anyone to share that look with. And never before had she wanted a brother or sister more than this moment.

Emma broke the eye contact and pushed up from her chair. "I need to start the meat pies for tonight."

As much as Monti hated to, she should leave the warmth of being tucked into Joseph's arm and go help his sister. This might be her only chance for a while to learn how to make meat pies.

She handed the guitar to Joseph. "I'll help, then I should start for home. I promised Antoine I'd be back before dark."

His finger stroked her arm as he helped her up. "Tell me when you're ready, and I'll saddle the horses."

She turned to study him. He'd only been here a few hours. Surely he'd planned to stay longer before he'd been roped into bringing her along. "You don't have to take me back. Stay here and visit with your family. I know my way home."

A line formed across his forehead. "There's too much danger in riding alone."

She raised her brows at him. "You do it all the time."

That line deepened as he scowled. "I have a gun, and I know how to protect myself."

"I have a gun, too. And I know how to protect myself." It was nice that he wanted to keep her safe, but she'd been independent long enough to be able to fend for herself.

His eyebrows shot up. "You have a gun? Where?"

She raised her chin. "In a place I'll not be showing, but you can be certain I have one and know very well how to use it."

He pressed his mouth together in a sure sign he was trying not to laugh. "Hmm... Well, be that as it may, I'll still ride back with you, if you don't mind. It'll help me sleep a mite better, so it's worth it to me."

She let out a sigh but kept from rolling her eyes. A few more hours alone with Joseph Malcom wouldn't be much of a hardship.

~

The day had been just about perfect. Maybe too close to perfect.

Joseph glanced at Monti riding beside him, surrounded by a sparkling landscape of newly-fallen snow. It still didn't seem possible that Monti knew about his hand and wanted him anyway. She acted as though it were nothing. As though it didn't create a gaping hole in his abilities, keeping him from so many things he used to do. Things other people took for granted.

Was she right? Overcoming his struggles didn't seem as easy as just...moving on. A simple decision. Maybe, little by little, his mind would get on board with this new reality. Was it his mind that had trouble grasping the facts? Somehow, the problem seemed a bit deeper. But now wasn't the time to analyze it.

Just enjoy these final two hours with Monti on their ride back to the priest's cabin.

"Tell your aunt and uncle I'm sorry I didn't get to come visit today." She glanced over at him, her eyes bright in a soft smile. "I'll look forward to seeing them next time."

He nodded. "Aunt Mary'll make sure you keep that promise." His feisty aunt was always eager for a visit.

A flash of movement in the snow caught his eye. Something big. He jerked back on his reins and threw out a hand to stop Monti.

A figure on horseback separated from the trees not more than two dozen feet ahead. An Indian mounted on a brown-and-white horse. Both the Indian's face and the horse's were marked with paint, and the brave wore several feathers standing upright in his hair.

Joseph scanned the woods behind the man, searching for more shadows moving among the trees. It didn't seem likely the man was alone.

No figures shifted among the barren branches, so he refocused his gaze on the brave approaching. With a jolt, recognition slapped him in the face.

Thunder Rumbles. This was the Indian who'd asked to marry Monti.

Joseph glanced sideways at her. She was staring at the man, too, eyes wide. Did she recognize him? She must, although he did look a bit different with a red circle painted around one eye and black lines under the other.

"Ride forward slowly," he muttered, just loud enough for her to hear.

She obeyed, then responded in a whisper, "I know him. He won't hurt us."

Wouldn't hurt *her* maybe, but the man was probably congratulating himself on this meeting. An opportunity to gain a new scalp and rid himself of the competition for Monti's affections, both at the same time.

They met the Indian and all reined to a stop. The man spoke the

Indian word for hello and signed, his gaze swinging from Joseph to Monti.

"Hello." Joseph made the same sign of greeting, but spoke in English so Monti would understand.

Thunder Rumbles didn't speak again, just stared at Joseph for a long moment, as though he were trying to read something in him. Deciding whether Monti was worth fighting over? No, that couldn't be it. One look at the woman confirmed the answer. What ran through the man's mind as those dark eyes drilled into him?

Joseph held his stare, keeping his back straight but his shoulders relaxed. He had no reason to feel inferior to this man. Well, at least no reason that Thunder Rumbles would know, not with the glove covering his crippled hand.

You only need be the man God made you to be. That's enough for me. Why Monti's words from the night before drifted through his mind at that precise moment, he had no idea. But they eased the twisting in his gut a little.

At last, the Indian nodded as though he'd settled something in his mind. He slid a glance to Monti again, then turned his horse and rode around them. No farewell or anything. His face as he passed didn't seem angry. Yet, not pleased either.

Monti let out a sigh after he'd ridden a short distance past them.

Joseph nudged Copper forward and motioned for her to ride on, too. They needed to get out of earshot before discussing the Indian. Many of the natives knew more English than they let on.

After a few minutes, Monti spoke in a loud whisper. "What do you think he wanted?"

Joseph glanced back, but Thunder Rumbles had disappeared from sight around a distant rock cropping. "I think he was just passing this way. I'm not sure why he was alone, though."

"I've never seen him painted like that. Did it mean he was going to battle?"

"Maybe just going to steal a horse or two. I don't think they have enemies in this area. They don't always get along with the Bloods, but the nearest band is the one you met several mountains over."

That seemed to give Monti enough to ponder, because she settled into silence for a while.

Their horses climbed a steep knoll, fighting through the snow so both animals breathed hard when they reached the top. Joseph reined in his gelding, and Monti did the same. "We'll let the horses rest for a minute. It's a pretty sight from up here."

The ground sloped downward, interrupted by the rock faces of three cliffs that rose almost straight up. "We call those The Triplets. All three mountains are almost impossible to climb except by the wild goats. Horses certainly can't climb them, but I think some of the Indian braves try during the rite of passage."

She glanced at him. "Have you ever tried?"

How did she know him so well already? He could feel his ears burning, but he was careful not to look at her. "I scaled the middle one last spring."

Her laugh tinkled out like a bell in the pure white of their snow-covered surroundings.

A movement to the side caught his eye, about halfway down the slope. Six deer wandered out from a copse of trees into the open.

He motioned toward them at the exact moment Monti gasped.

"Looks like there are two females, two babies, a young male, and a buck." He reached for his rifle in the scabbard.

"You're not going to kill one." Monti held a wounded tone.

"It'll give you and the priest fresh meat for a couple weeks." He sighted at the male sporting the huge rack of antlers, giving himself an extra few seconds to make sure he had the gun level in his bad hand.

Then he squeezed the trigger.

The explosion ripped the air with a flash and a cloud of black powder. The deer turned and bolted back the way they'd come. The buck ran only a couple strides before he went down.

Joseph's chest tightened, and he turned away. No matter how many times he did that, it wasn't any easier watching a living thing die. If only they could just go outside and retrieve their food from the ground each morning, like the Israelites had with the manna in the desert.

A look at Monti showed her biting her lip, a hand pressed over her heart.

"You stay here. I'll gather the meat and be back shortly." The last thing she needed was to watch him bleed out the carcass and hoist it onto the horse. Maybe he still had an oilskin in his pack he could wrap the body in so she didn't have to look at it.

She nodded. "Call me if you want me to come help."

He nudged his horse forward. "Just stay put. Don't move from this spot."

CHAPTER 19

Be Thou my Defender.
~ Monti's Journal

*M*inutes seemed to drag like hours as Joseph worked on the deer. The animal had a number of years on him and the hide was thick, which made everything harder. At least the work didn't require the fingers of both hands.

When he finally climbed back aboard Copper, the deer wrapped and tied on behind him, a half hour had passed. He nudged the horse into a trot, then a lope, as they ascended the slope.

The glare of the sun on the snow created a haze at the top of the knoll that looked almost like a cloud of fog. He'd seen this trick of the light before, though. He wouldn't be able to see Monti waiting patiently for him until he came within a few strides of her.

As Copper crested the hill, the glare faded, but Monti never came into view. Where was she?

He scanned the trail in both directions. "Monti?" His voice reverberated in the snowy silence.

No answering call. Only…his gaze lowered to the snow, which was churned in a wide swath that looked like a whole herd of horses had come through.

Bile churned in his stomach. Who'd been here? And where was Monti?

He raised his voice to a yell. "Monti!" His words echoed in the open spaces, and he held himself perfectly still as he waited for a reply. The air grew quiet and as still as a tomb.

A weight pressed hard on his chest as he pushed Copper forward to examine the tracks. None of the horses had been shod. Aside from the priest and Monti, the only others he knew who kept their horses unshod were Indians.

An image of Thunder Rumbles flashed in his mind. Had the Indian gone back and gathered more men to capture Monti and take her by force? The idea of her being held against her will nearly gagged him. It was a very real possibility. Even though that tribe was mostly peaceable, an Indian brave didn't take well to being thwarted. If he wanted Monti badly enough, Joseph had no doubt he'd take her by force.

The tracks seemed to travel back the way he and Monti had come, so he started riding that direction. It was hard to tell how many horses had been in the group. At least twenty, perhaps. Maybe more. Why so many? It would have been hard for Thunder Rumbles to gather such a large group quickly unless they'd already been assembled. Maybe he'd been riding with them but had separated for some reason when they'd seen him.

Joseph pushed his horse into a canter. It was easy enough to follow the tracks, and since Monti's mare wasn't shod, it would be impossible to decipher her prints from the others. He had to go on the hope and prayer that he was following the right trail.

Help me, God. If you ever choose to listen to my pitiful prayers, now is the time. Help me find Monti. He'd not prayed since the avalanche. That hour he'd been stranded with an awful weight crushing his hand, God hadn't seemed to care. At least, not enough to keep him from losing the use of five fingers. The Almighty had kept him alive but left him crippled.

The things that happened to you don't have the power to make you more or less than who you are. It's up to you to decide whether you'll live up to His plan for you. More of Monti's words, and as his chest thundered and he pushed his horse harder, the words seemed to thrash inside him. What was God's plan for him anyway? To lose everything that mattered in his life? First the use of his left hand, and now Monti.

He gave Copper a harder nudge, and the horse turned on a burst of speed. He had to find Monti. There was no telling what would happen to such a beautiful woman with no one to protect her. Especially with her feisty temperament thrown in the mix.

A shrill whistle pierced the air.

Joseph sat back in the saddle and searched the tree line ahead for the source as he eased Copper down to a walk. That had to have been a human sound. He'd never heard a bird make a call like that.

Then he showed himself. Thunder Rumbles rode out from the trees at a trot, straight toward him.

Joseph reached for his rifle. There was no telling what kind of trap this was, but he'd face it armed if he could. He aimed the gun at the Indian. "Where's Monti?"

The man slowed his horse to a walk but kept coming as if Joseph didn't have a firearm aimed at his chest. "Don't shoot." He made the sign for peace.

Peace, my eye. If the man hurt a hair on Monti's head, he'd not find peace anytime soon. He sighted down the barrel of the gun. "Where's Monti?" The man would know what he was asking by recognizing her name. There was no need to lower his gun to sign the question.

Thunder Rumbles stopped his horse with a dozen feet between them and began signing.

Joseph studied the motions. The sign language universal among most northern tribes was easier to learn than any of their individual languages, but he was still slow at it.

From what he understood, it looked like the Indian signed, *I know where the woman is.*

"Where is she?" He adjusted the gun again. The savage was

announcing that he had Monti? He must be planning to hold her for ransom. "What do you want for her? What is your price?"

A flash of confusion slipped across the Indian's face, and Joseph scrambled in his mind to find the Indian word for *price*.

But Thunder Rumbles began signing again. *Our enemies have taken her. I followed them a short distance, but they are many. We need more braves to fight them and take her back.*

"Your enemies?" Surely he hadn't read the gestures right. "You mean, the Bloods? The *Kainai?*"

The Indian nodded vigorously, then motioned Joseph forward. *Come. We need help to fight the enemy. Many braves to take the woman.*

Did he dare trust the man? He was pretty certain he'd read the signing correctly.

Thunder Rumbles waved him forward again, more urgent than stoic at this point. He was obviously impatient.

Do I go with him, Lord? If this were a trap, Joseph wouldn't have much chance for survival among a band of armed Indians. But what other choice did he have? And if it wasn't a trap, Monti could be in real danger among an enemy tribe. He could think of many reasons why they would want to capture her, and all of them made his gut churn and his heart race.

Determination sluiced through him, shoring up his uncertainty. He lowered the rifle but kept it pointed forward so he could use it with only a second's notice.

Then he nudged Copper forward. "Let's go.

~

*M*onti clung to the horn of her saddle, trying to keep some space between herself and the Indian whose arms formed a vise around her. More Indians on horseback drove their mounts like madmen, surrounding her and a handful of loose horses tucked in the middle of their circle.

It felt like they'd been riding at this speed for hours. Her insides had jolted until she jiggled like a soft pudding. Her sides ached, and so did the muscles through her arms and shoulders from hanging on.

She almost didn't have the energy to worry about where these men were taking her. And who were they? Dressed up in all the fancy furs and beadwork and feathers and wearing so much paint, it was almost impossible to tell for sure if she'd seen them before.

A few looked familiar. Maybe.

But familiar from Hungry Wolf's band of Peigan? Or had she seen these men when she traveled with Antoine to meet the tribe of Blood Indians over the mountains?

The tawny arms around her were solid as steel, keeping her from bouncing off the horse—and from any thought of escape. Of course, whether he rode with her or not, she wouldn't have much chance of getting away, surrounded as she was by at least twenty Indian warriors. And she'd not had a chance to reach for the gun hiding under her skirts.

At last, they came to a rocky trail that climbed upward, which required them to slow to a walk. The horses spread out single file, with some riders in the lead, others bringing up the rear, and the loose animals tucked sporadically in the middle. Dusk had fallen over the land, which meant darkness would soon be on them. She didn't recognize any of the mountains that now surrounded them on all sides.

"Where are you taking me?" She twisted to see her captor, the man who had leapt behind her on her horse as the Indians surrounded her. She'd been so focused on watching Joseph prepare the deer in the distance, she'd not heard the riders approach until too late. He'd been like a panther, this Indian, silent and lethal as he clamped one hand around her waist and another over her mouth. Her mare had bolted forward, and the rest of the men and horses fell into stride around them.

Now, he didn't respond at all to her question. He might not have understood. Or probably didn't care.

What had Joseph thought when he couldn't find her? He'd surely see the tracks. Would he try to follow?

A new fear clutched in her chest. He would follow. She had no doubt of that. But he'd be murdered in an instant if he tried to take on twenty Indian braves. *Lord, give him wisdom. Keep him safe.*

~

*T*he darkness was almost smothering.

With clouds covering the moon and stars, Joseph had to move slower than he wanted to follow the tracks. Even with so many hoofprints churning the snow, the shadows played tricks on his eyes until he could barely tell the difference between a snowdrift and a hoof mark.

Or maybe he was losing his mind.

It'd been about an hour since Thunder Rumbles left. He'd signed something about going back to get more men from his tribe, which would be helpful if it were true. It was hard to tell if the man was weaving a well-played trick and had Monti stowed away in his lodge even now, or if the distant tribe of Bloods really had kidnapped her.

Joseph had nothing to go on except these tracks and his senses.

And God.

The voice seemed to whisper in his mind. Part of him wanted desperately to pray for Monti. To turn her safety over to a God who cared and could be trusted to actually keep her unharmed. If only God would do that.

He'd not protected Joseph. Not kept his body whole through that agonizing hour buried under snow and rock.

But maybe…maybe He would do it for Monti.

God, do you care? She's come all the way out here for You. Will You protect her from harm? Please? For Monti's sake.

An image filled his mind of her dark, expressive eyes, smiling at him with those perfectly full lips. The flashing white teeth. Every feature refined to perfection. No porcelain doll was as beautiful as Monticello Bergeron.

And then his mind tried to imagine her bound and held tight by an Indian. A man with lusting eyes and plans to—

He forced his mind to clamp a lid on those thoughts before his anger took over. He had to focus.

A sound murmured in the darkness. A crunching of snow, perhaps? He reined Copper to a stop and turned in the saddle, peering for movement or shadows as he raised his rifle. The snow seemed to echo the faint noise so it was impossible to tell from which direction it came.

Could it be the Indians he was tracking? Maybe they stopped to camp for the night. He had to figure out where they were so he could sneak up on them. Maybe this was his chance to free Monti, even before Thunder Rumbles and his fellow braves arrived like a regiment of cavalry.

He slipped off his horse and led the animal to the side of the trail, off the wide swath of tracks. Maybe he should leave Copper here and move forward on foot.

The sounds of snow crunching seemed to grow louder. Then he heard the snuffle of a horse. Another nickered softly.

Joseph spun toward the noise. They were coming from his back-trail. Surely Thunder Rumbles hadn't returned so soon.

As Joseph waited just out of sight in the eerie darkness, the sounds grew louder. A group of riders, to be sure. Then the animals emerged from the blackness like spirits drifting from the dark place. Indians painted for war, feathers and war bonnets decorating their heads.

And there, front and center, rode Thunder Rumbles like the commanding general.

Should he step out and show himself? Or let them pass? If they were truly helping, he should join them. Maybe he'd learn more if he followed for a while. But why would Thunder Rumbles ride to find him if Monti hadn't actually been captured by enemy Indians?

He had to make a decision. Decide whose camp to join. Which side of the battle would he fight with? If only he could know for sure who was on his side. But there was no more time to ponder.

Before he could stop himself, he stepped forward, pulling his horse with him.

CHAPTER 20

I am more thankful than I can say for these unusual gifts.
~ Joseph's Journal

hunder Rumbles saw Joseph first and threw up his hand to
stop the others as he reined his horse to a nervous halt. He
motioned for Joseph to come forward and spoke a string of Indian
words.

Joseph stopped a half dozen strides before the man. He should say
something, but none of the Indian's language sprang to mind.

There was a stirring among the mounted Indians, and one of them
rode forward through the midst. Three Shadows. The man who'd
invited Joseph to join their hunt.

"Hello, Joseph." He knew a little English, speaking in a stilted
accent.

Joseph nodded at the man. "Three Shadows. I didn't expect to see
you all so soon."

The man made an angry gesture. "Our enemies steal horses. We
ride to fight. Find Thunder Rumbles. Hear of woman also stolen. We

ride with you." Another gesture like he was throwing a spear. Or maybe stabbing a knife into his enemy's heart.

We ride with you. The words rang through him like a rallying cry. They'd come to help him. To bring Monti back.

Certainty flooded his veins as he mounted Copper and turned to the Indians. "Let's go."

They rode for another hour as the trail wove through mountain passes and up rocky slopes. It was hard to recognize the landscape in the thick darkness, even though he'd ridden this country a hundred times at least.

Thank the Lord for the recent snow, they never had to worry over losing the tracks of their prey.

Thank the Lord. Did he really think the snow was a gift from God, given to aid their search? The snow did come from the Almighty, there was no question of that. But whether God sent it to help, well…maybe.

At last, Thunder Rumbles slowed his horse and raised a hand to halt the group. He spoke low in the Peigan tongue. The only word Joseph could decipher was *enemy.*

Three Shadows rode up beside Joseph, and he looked to the man for translation. "We near the enemy camp."

Thunder Rumbles spoke again, and Three Shadows interpreted. "We send two or three men to scout. See the enemy."

There was a general stirring among the men. Motioning.

"You should be among them." Three Shadows eyed Joseph.

Thunder Rumbles turned to look at Joseph, too. The man seemed to be studying him. Joseph met his gaze.

"I'll go with the scouts." Joseph eyed the man who'd wanted Monti as wife.

After a long moment, Thunder Rumbles spoke. Joseph couldn't make out any of the words, so it was good when Three Shadows translated.

"He said you should go. The woman would want it."

Thunder Rumbles held his gaze, then gave a single nod. A finale.

Giving him a distinct feeling the man had just conceded to Monti's wishes.

The group selected three of them to move forward alone—Joseph, Thunder Rumbles, and Three Shadows. They left their horses with the others and crept over the rocky terrain, around the base of a mountain. If memory served, the Indian camp should have been just around the jut in the rock, down in a ravine.

When they finally reached the point where the camp unfolded before them, they crouched to study the activity among the teepees. A few figures moved among the structures, outlined by the light of campfires. To the right, a group of horses milled restlessly. One animal squealed in the manner of horses just getting to know each other.

"Our horses." Three Shadows voice came out low and throaty. Dangerous.

"We have to find Monti first, then the horses." Joseph kept his voice low but firm. "Any idea where she is?"

Three Shadows translated, but before either of them could answer, two figures stepped from a lodge in the middle of the camp. Monti's long brown skirt and regal bearing were unmistakable. The brave walking behind her appeared to have a tight grip on her arm.

The Indian walked her toward another teepee, and they entered through the opening flap. That particular lodge was one row in from the outside of camp on the opposite side. If they could sneak around the camp and enter from that side, they might be able to get to the back of the lodge without being seen. Possibly.

"Should we try to sneak in? Or pretend to be one of them?"

Three Shadows shot him a skeptical look as he translated for Thunder Rumbles. Then he said, "You think you look Kainai?"

Joseph shrugged. "My sister's husband did it once to save her from the Apsalooke. He almost got away with it."

Three Shadows spat on the ground. "Apsalooke not have good eyes."

For just a second, Joseph fought a smile at his friend's obvious prejudice. But then the direness of the situation crashed over him, knocking the humor from him in a solid blow. He focused on the lodge where Monti and the Indian had entered. "So we sneak around the back?"

Thunder Rumbles shook his head, then turned to him and used his hands and sign language to outline a plan.

~

*O*f Monti didn't know better, she would have thought she was in Dashi's lodge again. The only thing missing was Hollow Oak lying on the pallet. From the animal-skin couch to the baskets of supplies and the stacks of bedclothes, everything seemed eerily familiar.

Every time she looked at the man sitting on the couch opposite her, dread crept over her arms and shoulders, slid down her back, and she had to force herself not to pull her coat tighter around her. A fire burned in the center of the dwelling, and a woman busied herself with what looked like food preparations against one wall. She sent Monti regular glances but hadn't spoken yet, at least not since she'd searched Monti and found her gun. There was no telling where that gun was now.

The man hadn't looked at her in a long time either. He just sat there, smoking his pipe and staring. After each inhale of the tobacco, he would pull the pipe aside and breathe a long stream of smoke toward her.

What did he intend? He was the one who'd swooped onto her horse and held her in his iron grip on the long ride to this place. He'd not let her out of his sight once in all those hours. Maybe after he ate whatever the woman prepared, they would all go to sleep and she could sneak away.

But as the hours passed, Indian after Indian entered to visit with the man smoking his pipe, even though her weary bones told her it had to be the middle of the night. The man seemed quite proud of himself, puffing out his chest as he spoke with his visitors, occasionally motioning toward her. They all seemed to speak with deference, as if he were an important man among them.

His position in the tribe only made the greedy glint in his proud gaze that much worse. What would he do to her? *Lord, let him wait until tomorrow. Give me escape tonight.*

The squaw had lain down on a pallet of furs, and now loud, steady breathing drifted from her.

Monti hadn't been able to bring herself to lie down, fearing she might not be able to keep herself awake. Exhaustion pulled so heavy at her eyelids and limbs. But maybe if she pretended, the Indian would stop staring at her and fall asleep himself. She tilted onto her side and closed her eyes.

He didn't at first, and she had to pinch herself over and over to keep awake. Especially with her eyes closed.

At long last, the man laid aside his pipe and stretched out on the furs beside the woman. She must be his wife. Did he also plan to take Monti as his wife? The thought made her stomach churn even worse, and her throat tightened until it was hard to get breath through. Many Indians had more than one wife. She'd learned that early on. Especially the chiefs. Yet, she couldn't imagine the idea. She knew nothing of this man.

Surely this couldn't be God's will for her life.

When the Lord saw fit to take her papa at such a young age—and right there in front of her—she'd come to terms with it. She and Mama had worked hard and become quite independent. And when that...that cad...had accosted her when she was fifteen, she'd overcome it. Learned how to protect herself so it could never happen again.

And then... Moisture surged to her eyes, unbidden, and she fought to send the tears back where they belonged. She'd finally stopped crying over Mama, and this wasn't the time to start again. Inhaling a long, silent breath, she focused only on the facts. Mama had passed. Monti had found a buyer for the business. It had all come together so smoothly.

The ease of wrapping up her life in Montreal had been one more sign to her that her spirit's urging to come join Antoine had been the Lord's will. Oh, she'd had a bit of trepidation about coming to such a wild, unsettled land. Would the Indians accept her? But not once had she ever truly questioned whether this was the place God wanted her.

She'd overcome so much. Endured. Fought with determination and tenacity and mental fortitude.

Had it all been for naught? *God, what did I do wrong?*

The battle is not yours, but God's. The words drifted through her mind like a whisper. Was that a verse from Scripture? Maybe.

The battle is not yours. Was God asking her to sit quietly and wait? The thought raised sheer panic in her chest. How could she not fight when the stakes were this high?

And then she remembered where the passage came from. Antoine had mentioned it just days ago when he'd shared the story of King Jehoshaphat. The Israelites had been preparing to go out to battle against a great army, and the Lord told them they would not need to fight in the battle.

Set yourselves, stand ye still, and see the salvation of the Lord with you, the verse had said. The thought had struck her as so unusual when Antoine described it. But Jehoshaphat hadn't questioned God at all. Not only did he tell the people not to fight, he commanded them to sing praises to the Lord during the battle.

And God had been true to His word. He'd made the enemies fight between themselves until not one person was left.

Could she trust that intensely? Sit quietly and wait for God to act? How long would that take? What if this Indian tried to take her...as his wife? Did she sit quietly and let that happen? *Oh, God.*

Rest in the Lord and wait patiently for him. Another passage from the Psalms.

"Dear Father." She whispered the words, building up her courage for what she had to say next. She had to. *I will wait for You, Lord. Fight my battle. Please.* She couldn't help tacking on that last part.

Kind of like the man in the Bible who reached out for Jesus to save his son. *Lord, I believe. Help thou mine unbelief.*

She tried to force herself to relax then. There was no reason to keep herself awake now, if she wasn't planning an escape.

But it was a long time before the tension eased from her muscles.

~

*J*oseph pressed his elbow on the bottom of the animal hide at the base of the lodge and worked his knife through the material. He had to jab hard to pierce the thick leather, then saw to widen the opening, which made his progress painfully slow. No matter what, he had to stay silent.

He could only pray the soft, steady breathing drifting through the animal-skins belonged to Monti and not some other woman. They'd studied the camp, found the guards stationed in strategic areas. Then watched this lodge for hours until finally the place seemed to quiet. Finally, they'd snuck around to the backside of the village, to the one place they could enter without meeting a guard.

He'd been the only one to creep through the camp to this teepee, though. It was up to him to get it right. Or he may very well die trying.

Let this be her, God. Please. Over the last few hours, he'd prayed more than ever, more even than during the avalanche. At first, he'd caught himself sending up quick prayers. But as the hours passed and he saw each successive man enter the teepee, his pleas had become more regular...and much more desperate.

God, if You'll just keep Monti safe and get her out of here, I'll do whatever you want. I'll take her place if you want me to. Or I'll make her go back to Montreal. The first time he said that, his chest threatened to close off his breathing. Could he really send her away? Maybe he'd go with her.

For now, better to focus on something he could actually commit to.

I'll be a better man, God. I'll read the Bible again. I'll settle down and stop wandering so much. Anything You ask. Just please, Lord, don't let them hurt her. Help me get her out of this place.

He finally cut through about four inches of the hide stretched over the lodge poles. Parting the slit, he bent low and peered through. The inside was dark with shadows concealing the details of each shape. After a minute or so, his eyes adjusted to the dimness.

Someone lay near him, as he'd suspected by the sound of steady breathing. A buffalo hide covered the form, but he could just make out the person's hair at one end. Dark. Was it black, like an Indian's, or lighter, like Monti's rich brown? The shadows made it impossible to tell.

And then, the person turned in her sleep, revealing the outline of a delicate profile against the faint glow of coals in the fire. That profile was emblazoned in his mind, those aristocratic features that had appeared in his dreams most every night.

With renewed fervor, he went back to cutting the leather covering. He didn't stay quite as silent this time, because it was Monti who lay nearest him. If she awoke, he only had to keep her quiet until he could sneak her out.

CHAPTER 21

My heart beats wildly.
~ Monti's Journal

*I*t must have taken an hour or more to cut a slice large enough for her petite frame to slide through. With no moon on this blackest of nights, he couldn't be sure what time it actually was. All he knew was they must be long gone by the time dawn brightened the sky.

Laying the knife aside, he reached his head and right arm inside the lodge, which was as much of him as the tiny opening would allow. He couldn't chance Monti waking with a start that might bring the others to life, so he slipped his hand over her mouth. Then he eased his thumb back and forth across her soft cheek.

He could feel the moment she awoke, her body tensing first, then her eyes easing open as though she were trying to calculate the danger before she showed too much awareness.

He didn't dare speak, but he shifted her head toward him so she would see who he was. The moment she saw him, her eyes popped wide. He eased his hand off her mouth and pressed a silencing finger to her lips. She nodded.

He scanned the room, then looked back at her and mouthed, "How many?"

She carefully pulled her hand out from under the fur and held up two fingers, then pointed over her shoulder across the lodge. The steady hum of a man's light snores made it apparent where one of the Indians was. He couldn't see the other.

He motioned for her to come out through the opening he'd cut, and she nodded understanding. As she lifted the buffalo robe and slipped out from underneath, the rustle of leather and fabric rumbled loudly in his ears.

He focused on the bulky mound across the teepee, but the only movement was a steady rise and fall of the shape.

Monti crawled toward him, and he pulled back out of the opening to let her through. She seemed to get snagged on something inside, and he heard a faint hiss, as though from pain. He couldn't see what the problem was, though.

Then she started toward him again, crawling barely above the ground.

Her head pushed through the opening. He tried to help pull her out, but she waved him away. It would probably be louder for him to pull her than for her to crawl herself. He'd never known a woman's skirts could make so much noise as they rubbed and rustled in the still of the night.

Finally, Monti had most of her body out. Then one leg. As she pulled the second leg free, her boot struck something that clanged like an empty tin.

She froze.

Something stirred inside.

He didn't wait any longer, just jerked her up and ran, bent low as they darted around a teepee toward the spot where Three Shadows and Thunder Rumbles waited.

A man hollered behind them. The shrill voice of a woman yelling. Dogs barked. A melee rose up, but Joseph ran, gripping Monti's arm in his hand. He'd left his knife back at the teepee. Lord willing, he wouldn't need it again until they were out of this mess.

Just as he rounded the front corner of a lodge, Monti cried out, and her arm almost jerked out of his grip. He swung around, preparing to fight whoever had grabbed her.

A giant of an Indian yanked her backward, but Joseph didn't let go. If he lost her, this beast of a man could turn and run.

He swung his leg up to deliver a hard blow to the man's lower regions. He wasn't above playing dirty. Monti's life was at risk here.

The man grunted but never lost his hold on his captive. A swish sounded, and a glint of metal shone in his hand.

He raised the knife high, but another scream pierced the air. This one a war cry.

A blur rushed by Joseph from behind.

Thunder Rumbles raised a lance and thrust its end into the brute.

The man released Monti's hand, and she jerked back and away from him.

The two Indians launched into hand-to-hand combat. The stranger had blood spewing from his shoulder, and Thunder Rumbles seemed to be quickly overtaking him.

"Let's go!" Joseph yelled. He didn't have to pull hard for Monti to follow, and she was on his heels as they reached the spot where Three Shadows waited, crouching.

The man rose at their approach. "Where is the other?"

"He's fighting the Indian." Joseph could barely draw enough breath to speak. "He needs help. Get Monti out of here and I'll go back." Thunder Rumbles had saved their lives. Joseph had to get back and help him.

Three Shadows pulled out his knife. "Take her and call for the others. Don't wait for us. Our men will fight the battle. Take the woman to her people."

Joseph paused, emotion clogging his throat. "I can't leave you."

The other man met his gaze. "Yes. Take her to safety." He clasped Joseph shoulder.

He swallowed down the burn in his throat. "Thank you." *For everything.* "Go. Thunder Rumbles needs you."

With that, the Indian disappeared into the darkness.

For the first time, Joseph let himself turn and look at Monti. She looked so tired. So fragile beside him. He still clutched her arm, but he let his hand loosen and slide down to take her hand, weaving their fingers together.

What he really wanted was to pull her close, but they weren't safe yet. He had to get her out of there and summon the other men. "Can you run?" He met those dark, breath-stealing eyes.

She nodded. "Wherever you lead."

He kept a hold on her hand while they ran, darting from shadow to shadow as they made their way through the narrow space between the camp's edge and the cliff wall. Monti didn't drag behind, but the going was slower than if he were by himself. They were moving away from the commotion, thank God.

The brawl had grown louder, which tightened the knot in his gut when he thought about Thunder Rumbles and Three Shadows trying to hold their own against all those Indians. He had to get help.

The pounding of hooves sounded in the opposite direction from camp, and even in the darkness, he knew exactly who it was. The other braves must have heard the noise or grown worried when the escape took so long.

No matter the reason, the cavalry had arrived. With twenty mounted warriors, they all stood a strong, fighting chance of coming out of this skirmish alive. And maybe even with the horses that had been stolen.

He tightened his grip on Monti's hand. "My horse is a little farther."

He couldn't see her face in the darkness, but he could feel her answering squeeze. "Lead on."

~

*M*onti clung to the saddle horn as Joseph pushed his horse to keep up the quick pace. The blush of dawn was lightening the eastern sky, and they'd been riding pell-mell for what felt like a half hour at least.

But she didn't blame him for wanting to get as far away as possible before they slowed. Even though her lower regions were growing numb from all this time in the saddle, she couldn't complain about being tucked inside his strong arms. The arms that made her feel safe and cherished. He kept his left arm around her waist while he used the other hand to steer.

And every so often he'd lean forward and murmur something like. "I prayed you'd be safe." Or, "I can't believe you're all right. Are you sure you're not hurt?"

Yes, he made her feel cherished.

It was another quarter hour before Joseph finally let the horse slow to a walk.

She leaned forward and stroked the gelding's reddish-brown winter-thick hair. "You're a good boy, Copper. I'm sorry to make you work so hard all night."

"He'd do a lot more if it meant keeping you safe and getting you back." Joseph's deep tenor rumbled in her ear.

She turned to smile at him and couldn't help a bit of teasing. "Are you speaking for the horse or yourself, Monsieur Malcom?"

The way his eyes darkened to rich chestnut nearly stole her breath. She could melt in those eyes, especially when they heated with the intensity blazing in them right now. "For the horse. As for me, there's nothing I wouldn't do for you. I promised God, too."

Then he leaned forward and brushed a warm, breathy kiss on her jaw.

And the shiver that coursed through her at that touch was enough to steal the strength from her limbs. She lay against the cradle of his arm and turned her face to him fully.

If it were possible, his eyes darkened even more. His kiss was feather-soft, sugar sweet, and oh... She had no power to do anything but revel in him.

Joseph.

This man who'd taken her heart so fully. He brought parts of her to life she didn't know she possessed. The man who'd first cracked her defenses, letting her see she didn't always have to be self-sufficient. Softening her heart so the Lord could reach through and take over. Fight her battles.

And just as He'd promised, His salvation had been swift and complete.

~

*M*onti was asleep in Joseph's arms when he reined his horse to a stop in front of Emma's cabin. Weariness had seeped all the way through his bones, and he wasn't altogether sure he could hold them both up if he ever got them off the horse.

The cabin door opened, and Simeon appeared, still pulling on his coat as if he were on his way out to tend the animals. He looked surprised to see them and turned to speak to someone inside before he closed the door and trotted down the step, still adjusting his coat.

"What's wrong?" The concern on his face was obvious.

What a sight they must look, weary and bedraggled and probably quite tousled. Monti, of course, was beautiful as always, but not her usual put-together self. "It's a long story. Need to get her inside and warm. She'll need a meal and sleep, too."

Monti woke then, shifting and mewing like a sleepy kitten. It made him want to snuggle her tight and nuzzle her jaw and the softness of her neck. But he would restrain himself...for now.

She let Simeon help her down, then looked up at Joseph.

He dismounted and slipped a hand around her waist so he could speak into her ear. "Go inside and let Emma fuss over you. I'll be in as soon as I tend Copper."

"I'll take the horse." Simeon reached for the reins. "You both go get warm."

The cabin door opened, and Emma came out in a flurry, seconding her husband's words.

Joseph didn't try to fight it, just asked Simeon to give his gelding an extra ration of feed and put the deer carcass in a safe place. Emma had her hand tucked in Monti's elbow, so he let his grip slide away from her waist. But then she reached for his hand, weaving her fingers through his like she'd done on the ride. Making his chest hitch.

Somewhere during the night—maybe during the fear that dogged his ride to the Indian camp, maybe when he saw her elegant profile lying on the pallet of furs in the Indian lodge, or maybe when he held her tight on the hurried ride to safety. Somewhere, he'd made a decision, deep in the innermost parts of him.

God had brought this woman into his life. A blessing he'd never expected. Even when the Almighty had practically wrapped the gift in a fancy bow, he'd tried to hand it back.

No more. He would accept the gifts he'd been given. The grace. Monti.

He'd accept and treasure them.

CHAPTER 22

No longer I, but Christ within me.
~ Joseph's Journal

*M*onti had to force her eyelids open as her body awoke, and, for just a moment, she thought she was still on the trail with Joseph. That first journey from Fort Hamilton to Antoine's cabin. Her muscles ached like they had during those long days in the saddle, but this straw tick and colorful quilt had definitely not been with them on the trail.

She stretched, letting herself enjoy the luxury of Emma's spare bed chamber for another stolen moment.

Voices hummed in the other room, and she glanced at the window. Daylight. The lighting seemed dim, like it was either morning still or coming into evening. Either way, she'd better get moving.

The events with the Indians seemed like another lifetime. Or maybe part of her dreams.

A thought jolted her. Antoine. She'd not returned home last evening. He must have been frantic.

After lacing her boots, she moved toward the door and opened it, taking a moment to peer out into the main room. Several people sat around the table, and the moment she took in the slightly stooped shoulders of her father's cousin, her pulse slowed. Someone must have ridden to tell him she was safe.

Then her gaze landed on a form sitting opposite the priest. Joseph. He was looking at her with one side of his mouth tipped up in that grin that roused a fluttering in her midsection. Maybe it was the dark stubble on his jaw that gave him the aura of a rogue. Regardless, the sight of him made her chest tighten and pulled an answering smile from her.

"Monti." Emma rose from her chair to stride toward the stove. "Come eat with us. I made a thick stew. You must be starved. And you've come out early enough that Joseph hasn't eaten it all yet."

Antoine stood and turned to her, his arms out. She moved into them, letting the warmth of his fatherly embrace soothe the rough ends of her fractured nerves.

"I knew our Father would care for you, ma fifille. But I must say, I kept my petitions at his feet all through the night." His weathered voice seemed to quiver a bit.

She gave him an extra squeeze. "He fought the battle for us. But I've never been so happy to wake in a bed as I was just now."

He patted her shoulder, then motioned toward the empty chair beside Joseph. "Sit and eat."

She met Joseph's gaze as she walked around to the empty chair, and when she sat, the way he squeezed her hand under the table sent a flow of warmth up her arm.

The meal saw a lively conversation as she recounted her story, and Joseph filled in with tidbits from his own adventures. Apparently, he'd been awake long enough to have told the full version of his tale to the group already. He'd already told her those details as they rode last night. She could still feel him sitting behind her in the saddle, arms strong around her, breath warming her neck as his deep vibrato rumbled in her ear.

"I wish I hadn't gone for that deer." That same gentle tenor soothed her, even now.

"If you hadn't, those Indians might have scalped you to get Monti. Then where would you both be?" Emma eyed her brother from the end of the table. The stubborn lift of her chin and the narrowed glare of her amber eyes was a look that seemed familiar. The same look she'd seen on Joseph more than once.

He shrugged and turned to Monti. His gaze seemed to thicken in a way that melted her insides as his thumb stroked her hand under the table. "I just wish none of it had happened."

It was hard to form a coherent thought with Joseph looking at her that way, much less put it into words. Yet she forced herself to give voice to the insight she'd had as she drifted to sleep in Emma's cozy bed. "They meant it for my harm, but God meant it for good."

"Oui." Antoine straightened in his chair and looked at her. "Are you ready to go home, ma fifille?"

A twinge of something she'd rather not define pinched her chest, but she ignored it and nodded. "I am." She could make the journey again. And this time she would be on her guard.

"I'm coming with you." Joseph spoke with a stubbornness in the line of his jaw that brooked no discussion.

She bit back the impulse to mention that he'd ridden with her last time when she was kidnapped. Of course, it wasn't his fault she'd been taken. And besides, Joseph wasn't her protector, God was. It was nice when God used him for the job, though.

The ride back was blessedly uneventful, and they reined in at Antoine's little cabin just as dusk was turning into full darkness.

"You must stay the night with us." Antoine spoke to Joseph as he dismounted.

"Of course." She offered Joseph a hopeful smile as she handed over her reins. The men would be cold and hungry, so her time would be better spent starting a fire than unsaddling her horse. This time, at least.

"I suppose so. If it's not too much trouble."

The flutters in her middle took flight again at the thought of a few more hours with Joseph.

∼

*T*he next morning, Joseph couldn't get his nerves to settle. He'd planned to take Monti out for a ride as soon as the day warmed, to ask the question burning in his chest.

But maybe he was crazy. What right did he have to ask a woman like her to shackle herself to a cripple like him?

With the worry dogging him, he rose early and went out to hunt for breakfast. Monti seemed happy as a puppy let out to play when he handed her the fresh meat an hour later, and it was only her gentle smiles through the morning meal that calmed the knot in his belly.

As soon as he could, he excused himself and stepped out for a bit of a walk in the chilly air. He had to recover some of the certainty he'd felt the morning before. It was time for that talk with God he'd promised he'd do each day. In truth, something inside him yearned for it.

The snow-covered landscape still looked new and clean from the fresh coat of white that had fallen two days before. Had it only been two days since he'd accompanied Monti to visit his sister? His emotions had been so unsettled then. Happiness that Monti didn't seem bothered by his useless hand. Yet, a part of him had felt like there was something still missing.

He'd discovered the missing part.

Now, he stared up at the sky, an endless blue not marked by puffy white clouds. God was up there, looking down even now.

And, lo, I am with you always, even unto the end of the world. The words came to him as though spoken out loud. That was from the Bible, a passage he'd memorized long ago.

He raised his face to the warmth of the morning sun, letting his eyes drift closed. "I know, God. I see it now. I'm going to need help, though." He'd been so submerged in his misery these past months, he had a feeling it would take a lot of leaning on God to carry him forward.

Opening his eyes, he breathed in as a breeze ruffled his hair. Peace. He'd not known it in so long, yet he could feel it now. Sweet relief.

He glanced around, taking in the snowbirds hopping through the cluster of dormant vines near him. "What now, God?" Should he carry on with his plans to ask Monti?

One of the birds bounced up beside another, twittering and cocking its head. The other animal waddled forward to close the distance between the two, then rubbed its head against the shoulder of the first bird.

He didn't move as the animals seemed to almost embrace in an intimacy he'd never seen before from birds. Hadn't God said it wasn't good for man to be alone? Not good for animals, nor for people.

He raised his face to the heavens again. "All right. I'll ask, but you'll have to make her say yes."

As he walked back toward the cabin, he almost let himself imagine what it would be like if Monti accepted his marriage proposal. Soon. He would ask her very soon.

～

*M*onti eyed Joseph out of the corner of her eye as they rode side-by-side.

When he'd returned from his walk, he seemed different. Lighter, somehow, and determined. As though he'd settled something in his mind and was ready to get on with it.

And now, he wouldn't tell her exactly where they were riding to. He'd just said he wanted to show her something.

He caught her look and smiled the kind of grin she hadn't seen on his face very often. The look that said he had a secret and was bursting to tell her.

Maybe...perhaps she could use the womanly wiles she'd been blessed with to get it out of him. Or maybe she'd just sit back and enjoy the outing with him.

They didn't ride far, just about a quarter hour before Joseph reined to a stop at the opening to a small valley. It was flanked by a cliff on one side and a low hill on the other. Near the hill sat a line of trees that probably contained a creek, if she were to guess based on what she knew about the landscape in this area.

The whole valley seemed a natural enclave, a haven of peace.

Joseph sat at the entrance staring out over the land with a wistful expression on his face.

"This is nice, isn't it?" She raised her chin as a gentle breeze brushed her face.

He looked over at her. "You think so?"

"I do." She met his gaze with a smile.

He nodded, as though her words had settled something in his mind. Then he nudged his horse forward. "Come on. I want to show you something."

As she followed him into the valley, the sun seemed to warm the place more than it had outside the shelter of the mountains. He rode toward the trees, then dismounted when they reached the edge of them.

He came forward to help her down, but she slid off her horse before he could reach her. As they tied the horses to branches, she peered through the dimness of the trees. "Is there a stream in there?"

"There is. It might be frozen, though. I haven't been here in a couple months."

She started to step into the woods, but he grabbed her hand as she walked by him. "Wait a minute. I want to ask you something first."

The edge in his voice made her pause and search his face. Lines had formed under his eyes as if he'd not slept well.

"What is it, Joseph?" She stepped forward and pressed both of her palms to his chest. If only she could slip her arms around him and take away all his worries.

He rested his hands on her elbows, then stroked his palms up her arms and around her back, leaving a warm heat everywhere he touched, even through the layers of her coat and clothing.

She kept her focus on his face, waiting for him to explain. His brow had puckered, and he seemed to be preparing his words. Or maybe thinking through whatever had him so uptight. "What is it?" She knew better than to press, but surely they could solve the problem better together.

He met her gaze then, his eyes a clear amber that seemed to look through to her very soul. "Will you marry me, Monti?"

The question hung in the air as she tried to absorb it.

"I know I—" He stopped short. "I—" Again he stalled, as though biting down on his words. His face scrunched as if the taste of them were sour.

She wanted to jump in, to laugh and say, *yes, a thousand times yes!* But something inside made her keep silent. He needed to speak whatever made him hesitate.

At last, he let out a long breath and met her gaze again. "You're so extraordinary. It's hard to imagine you'd say yes, but I'm asking. I still have so much work to do on myself, but with God's help, I'll get there. And I can promise you, I'll work 'til my dying breath to be the man you deserve."

His words tightened an ache in her chest, and she raised one hand up to cup his cheek. "You only need be the man God made you. That's enough for me." She'd said those words before, but she'd never meant them as much as she did now. And she'd say them a thousand times again if they helped. "And, yes. I can't think of a greater honor than to become your wife."

His gaze turned hopeful. Earnest. But he still had those worry creases under his eyes. "Are you sure? You can say no."

She gave him a dramatic sigh and stretched up on her toes. "You're impossible." She pressed her gloved hands to each of his cheeks and stared into his eyes. "I didn't plan to marry. Didn't want to, until I met you. You make me see that there's more to life than what I can do myself. Sometimes, I have to let others in." She pulled his forehead down to hers, and she breathed him in. "I want to let you in."

Then she slipped her hand behind his neck and pulled him closer for a kiss.

His mouth was warm on hers, his kiss a gentle caress that sent warm tingles all the way through her. But then he came back for a second, then another. Each one infused with a passion that awakened her senses, pulling her closer, lighting her on fire.

He stopped long before she was ready, pulling back only a little until his forehead rested on hers. Their breath mingled, warming her already heated face. Making her want to pull him close again.

But instead, she let herself relish the feel of him. The nearness of him. *Oh, Lord. You've been good to me, indeed.*

"I never dreamed God would be so good to me." His voice was a husky murmur, and his words brought a smile to her face that stretched her cheeks.

"That's exactly what I was thinking." And she snuggled in closer.

CHAPTER 23

This gift I never thought I wanted...I now can't imagine life without.
~ Monti's Journal

TWO MONTHS LATER

*J*oseph straightened, clasping his hands in front of him as his sister stepped from the cabin. His chest thumped loud enough he could hear it in his ears. But when she closed the door behind her, the knot that had formed in his midsection over this last half hour of waiting pulled tighter. Had Monti changed her mind?

Emma walked toward him with purposeful steps, and if it weren't for the slight tipping up of her lips, he might have charged forward to take her by the shoulders and shake her. Where was Monti?

His sister didn't speak as she marched across the expanse of grass and through the cluster of Indians who'd become friends over the past two months. Hollow Oak reached out to her, and Emma stopped to tweak one of the girl's braids, receiving a beaming smile in return. Thank God, the remedy Simeon had put together seemed to be helping the girl. Although she still grew short of breath easily, she'd not been ill enough to stay abed since she recovered from her fall on the ice. And the swelling seemed greatly reduced in her limbs.

The girl's mother stood behind her, hands resting on her little shoulders. Fighting Elk seemed like a sentry beside his little family, and a short distance away, Thunder Rumbles stood with his arms crossed over his chest. His feet spread in the stance of a warrior.

As Joseph met the man's gaze, he had to swallow down the lump in his throat. This Indian brave had proved deserving of the word *brave*. The night he'd stepped in to help Joseph save Monti, the man had shown a courage and selfless valor few could boast. Thank God none of his Peigan comrades had been mortally wounded. They'd even recovered most of the stolen horses.

And over the weeks Thunder Rumbles had come to help Joseph build this cabin, Joseph had come to respect the man even more.

Thunder Rumbles now held his gaze, and the corners of his mouth slipped up a tiny bit.

Thank you, friend. Hopefully Joseph's gaze spoke his thoughts.

The other man nodded.

Emma proceeded past the Indians and now stopped before him, less than a foot away. He searched her eyes, trying to read the truth in them. He'd always been able to read Emma's mind, and usually her heart, too.

Now, what he saw reestablished that lump in his throat.

She reached up and cupped his cheek, then stretched up on her toes and kissed his freshly shaved jaw. "I'm proud of you, Joey." Her words were a whisper, meant only for him. "I wouldn't be able to give you up if I didn't know you'd be happy."

He wrapped his arms around her. His twin. Pressing his face in her hair, he breathed in the gift God had blessed him with. One of the many. One of the most special. "I know it." His eyes burned, and he took in a breath to clear them.

Then he set Emma back so he could look into the eyes that

matched his exactly. "You're not losing me, though. In fact, I think I've finally been found."

She smiled through glimmering eyes, then sniffed and stepped back.

And that was the exact moment the door to his cabin opened—his new cabin. The one tucked in the valley with the stream. The one he would share with Monti.

She stepped from the house and turned to face him. In her yellow gown with the flowers and lace, she was the image of a French princess. Soon to be *his* French princess.

She walked toward them, a bouquet of holly branches in her hands, the only flowers to be found in the northern winter. Yet nothing could dim her beauty. The way she glowed as she neared, her eyes shining. Her smile dazzling. Her face tilting up toward him.

He reached for her, taking her hand as they neared. Even as they turned to face the priest, his dear friend Antoine, Joseph couldn't quite pull his eyes away from her.

Who would have thought a simple errand to fetch the priest's cousin would bring him back to life? And this life, full of so many mercies from God, was better than anything he could have imagined.

EPILOGUE

Bone of my bone.
~ Joseph's Journal

*J*oseph stared out over the valley, then to the snowcapped peaks stretching as far as he could see, rising into the heavens. He could never quite get enough of the view here. The wild beauty of this land still had the power to fascinate him.

Soft footsteps approached from behind, and he turned to see the face whose delicate features still made his heart leap every time he looked at her. His French princess. The sun shone on her russet-colored hair, framing her smile with its golden rays.

He reached for her, and she came to him, settling in front of him to look out over the majestic mountains she claimed to love as much as he did. He wrapped his arms around her, pressing a kiss to her hair as she leaned back against her. This...was perfect. Truly.

"I can't imagine a moment more perfect." Monti's voice held a wistful tone that matched the longing in his chest.

He couldn't help but chuckle. "You read my thoughts again."

She glanced up at him, and he took the opportunity to take her lips in a quick kiss. Just to remind her how much she was loved.

When she straightened, she settled her hands over his, then moved his right hand lower on her swelling middle. "The little one's enjoying the moment, too. Do you feel that?"

He kept himself perfectly still, every nerve straining to sense movement under his hand. "I think... Was that a kick?" The touch was almost a flutter, like nothing he'd ever felt before. A thrill surged through him at the thought of the new life growing inside her. The life they'd both helped create. It all still seemed too much to fathom. Too wonderful.

She turned her face to him again, a smile spreading across her lovely face. "Isn't it wonderful?"

He couldn't help another kiss on that upturned mouth. "My thoughts exactly."

Did you enjoy Joseph and Monti's story? I hope so!
Would you take a quick minute to leave a review?
It doesn't have to be long. Just a sentence or two telling what you liked about the story!

~

And would you like to receive a **free short story about a special moment in Gideon and Leah's happily-ever after**?
Get the free short story and sign-up for insider email updates by tapping here.

I pray you enjoyed Joseph and Monti's story! Here's a peek at the next book in the series, *This Freedom Journey*. This is a novella (meaning a half-length novel) that tells the story of Aunt Mary and Uncle Adrien—back when they first met.

Here's a quick peek at the first chapter. Enjoy!

This journey I take seems foolish to others, yet I can't help the yearning that fuels me.
~ Adrien's Journal

January, 1833
Rupert's Land, Canadian Territory

Adrien Lockman trudged through the snow, the frames of his snowshoes carrying him at least two feet higher than the weary mule tracking behind him. Mountains rose on either side, but this narrow gap between the rock cliffs kept the wind from badgering them. Much.

Maybe he should try to build a shelter between these mountains to spend the rest of the winter. Protection on two sides was better than nothing. And he'd have access to the hot springs he'd stumbled on the day before. Water any time he needed, even though the stuff smelled murky.

But something drove him onward. Maybe the fact that these winter months were the last chance he would allow himself to explore unfettered. When spring came, he'd be building a house in that wide valley he'd found a couple days before. That open land spread far enough to raise a host of cattle and horses. Live life on his own terms. He'd have responsibilities, but the kind of his own choosing.

Until then, he planned to cover as much ground as he could. Explore as far into these great rocky peaks as his snowshoes would take him.

Wind gusted against his face, blowing up a cloud of icy pellets covering the ground. At least only a little snow was falling from the sky today.

He pulled his fur cape higher over his face so only a slit for his eyes was open to the elements. As he pushed on, the wind battered more, blowing its cold fury to sting his eyelids.

The blinding white swirled around him, thick enough so the cliffs beside him vanished. How much fell from above and how much was blown up from below became impossible to decipher. The brutal icy air churned like a dense cloud restricting his ability to judge distance.

Should he stop and wait for the wind to die down? The biting cold had benumbed his limbs, giving him little choice. He wouldn't last much longer in these fierce elements without shelter.

He continued forward and to the right, reaching out to feel the cliff side before he ran into it. Poor Domino trudged behind him, soldiering on. The reluctant mule must have resigned himself to freezing to death some time yesterday, when he'd stopped balking at the belly-high snow.

After a dozen strides, Adrien's hand still hadn't struck the wall of mountain that spanned them on the right. Perhaps the cliff had tapered to a low hill at this point. The snow swirled thick—so thick he could only make out objects a few feet ahead.

He stopped, then turned to his left toward the cliff that held court on that side of the narrow trail. He progressed a dozen strides that way. Where was the mountain?

The first solid stab of fear twisted in his chest.

Oh, God. Have mercy on me.

He had to find one of those cliff walls. Or maybe the cliffs were gone now, and the land had opened into a valley. He might never find shelter. To this point, the snowy wilderness had been an adventure. But in this freezing blizzard, with no barriers around him to tame the torrent of wind and snow, he might very well freeze to death before nightfall.

His mother had predicted the territories would eat him alive. *God, please don't let her be right.*

No sudden stillness split the howling wind in answer to his prayer. Nor did he feel a voice inside him giving direction on how to save himself.

But he had to do something. He couldn't stand here wishing for sunshine while his body turned to an ice block.

He turned back to Domino, stroking under his ice-encrusted forelock. The mule blinked snowy lashes at him.

"We'd best keep walking. I'd rather die doing something than standing still."

He adjusted his position to what should be straight forward on the trail between the mountains. Unless the blizzard had his senses more off-kilter than he'd thought—a deadly possibility.

Pushing off on his snowshoes, he tried to keep going in a straight line. A minute passed, but the going was slow with the wind beating against him and his spirits plunging.

He should start singing. The only song that came was that rowdy barroom tome that had played over and over from the building beside his hotel in Quebec. He'd hated the song then, but maybe today the tune could help him survive.

He forced out the lyrics to "A Lady of High Degree." The effort to move his cracked lips caused them to ache, but at least pain meant he was still alive.

Halfway through the second verse, a wooden blur appeared ahead of him. Adrien squinted, trying to discern the shape. A building?

Dragging his snowshoe-laden feet forward, he moved close enough to touch the icy surface, his thick leather gloves meeting solid wood.

A surge of energy flooded him. His imagination hadn't fooled him. He'd actually found a building.

Charging forward, he ran his hand along the rough wall as he searched for a door or other opening. The logs stretched about four strides before turning a corner. He followed them around and, finally, found the door.

Closed.

He fisted his hand and banged on it. Surely there wasn't a person living out here, so far from any fort or trading post. He'd felt like he was the only man alive for days.

The wind howling around him covered any sounds that might come from inside. No latch string hung out as a sign that visitors could enter, but surely whoever had built the cabin wouldn't mind him taking shelter from the blizzard.

He pushed his shoulder into the door. The wood wiggled as if it weren't very strong, but the barrier didn't open. He could break through with one good kick, probably.

Best try knocking first, though. Before he could raise a fist, the door swung wide.

Adrien straightened, peering into the darkness. Who had opened it?

An animal shifted inside, big and hairy. Like a bear. Or...a buffalo?

Adrien pulled Domino closer so he could reach the rifle strapped on the mule, yet he couldn't take his eyes from the creature before him. The head shifted, and a bit of pale skin appeared.

A person's face?

His breath left him in a whoosh, and he inhaled again, trying to still his thundering heart.

"What do you want?" The voice inside the fur robe yelled over the howling wind, but not even the blizzard was loud enough to disguise the high tone.

A woman?

Domino nudged his side, pulling him from the shocking discovery. He had to get them out of the wind. He jerked down the muffler that covered his mouth and inhaled to force out words.

Before he could speak, the woman swayed, first one direction, then toward the door as she clung to the wood for support.

"Are you well?" He reached out. The dim light and that dark fur shrouding her made her face seem as pale as death. He stepped forward to help her—or tried to, but his snowshoe caught on the wood transom beneath the door.

He pitched forward but caught himself on the frame.

She swayed again, and he reached out for her, but too late. Her eyes rolled back in her head, and she fell to the dirt floor.

Raising his legs high so the awkward frames cleared the doorway, he stepped inside and glanced about. Nothing moved inside the small cabin.

The place was only one dim room with a rough-built fireplace and chimney at one end. No fire in the hearth. A pile of furs lay in the corner like a sleeping pallet. That would be the best place to put her.

He pushed the door shut to block out the wind, then eased down in front of the woman and pulled the fur cape back from her face. Dark brown hair spilled over her cheek. Her skin blanched almost as white as the snow outside. He shifted her so he could find an acceptable place to put his hands to carry her.

Her closed eyelids never moved. Heavens, don't let her be dead.

She hung limp in his arms as he clomped to the stack of furs, and he tried to cradle her head in the crook of his elbow.

He sank to his knees to lay her on the low pallet, and she stirred as he pulled his hands out from under her. Thank the Lord she wasn't dead.

She didn't open her eyes, though.

"Mademoiselle." He pulled off a glove and reached to touch her forehead. A glance at his bright red fingers stilled him. His skin was so icy he may not be able to feel whether she was feverish. But maybe they'd jolt her senses enough to wake her.

He pressed his hand to her brow. His brawny skin appeared so rough and masculine next to the pale softness of her features.

Her lashes fluttered. Long, black lashes that raised to reveal a sliver of blue. Her gaze seemed sleepy as it swept in a slow arc. When her focus lifted to his face, her eyes widened, and she came to life. Her muscles tightened under his hand, and she pulled back.

He jerked away, scooting backward to give her more space. Except the snowshoes wouldn't let his feet move where he commanded. His body obeyed, however, shifting backward without anything to hold him up.

He toppled to the floor, landing on the raised edge of his snowshoe. The ache in his backside would leave a bruise tomorrow. He glanced at the woman to see if she'd caught his less-than-graceful retreat.

She lay there, rounded eyes luminous against her delicate features as she stared at him. She spoke, but the words came in English, and the only sound he could decipher was "Who."

Pushing up to a crouch, he worked his snowshoes backward to give her a bit of space. Then he focused on the woman again and spoke in his native tongue. "I only speak French. My name is Adrien Lockman."

Her brows knit in a thoughtful expression. Not complete confusion as he'd expected. Maybe she understood a bit of the language. He pressed on, keeping his words slow and as clear as he could make them with his mouth still frozen. "You are unwell. What can I get you for your relief?"

She started to sit up, but the way her face scrunched and her mouth pinched, the effort proved too difficult.

"Lie still." He wanted to reach out and ease her back down, but something about the wariness in her eyes put him in mind of a cornered wildcat. "I won't hurt you. I mean only to help. What is your name?"

She gave up trying to rise. Something must be truly wrong with her if she was that weak. Her gaze arrowed a seething glare his way. "What is your business here?" She spoke in French, although halting and stilted.

He glanced over his shoulder at the closed door, the wind still howling outside. "I grew lost in the blizzard and almost ran into your cabin. I was hoping you would shelter my mule and me until the snow stops." He ran his gaze over her face, drawn and pale. "It's good I came when I did. You are not well. What can I get for you? Water to drink? Maybe a broth? Have you any stew or meat I can simmer?"

She shook her head. "There's water by the hearth. I don't need food. Let me rest and I'll be well."

He glanced at the hearth where a pot which probably held the water sat. Then he slid his gaze around the rest of the room. Sparse. Really, there was almost nothing else there. Not even scraps of wood to build a fire. Did that mean she didn't have food either? That would certainly explain her weakened state.

Rising to his feet, he took a step back so he wouldn't tower over her. "Do you mind if I bring my mule inside? Only until the wind settles down."

She nodded. "Bring him."

Thank you, Lord. Once he had Domino settled, he'd get a fire going and heat some food for her. Beans would be warm and stick to her belly, but maybe he'd start with something quicker. He could parboil a bit of venison. She didn't look like she'd last long enough for the beans to cook without something to hold her over.

Within minutes, he had his snowshoes off and a fire licking at the dried wood he'd stored in Domino's pack. The oilskin had kept all his supplies nice and dry, despite the blizzard.

Domino let out a bray as he sniffed the interior of the cabin. If the place had a wood floor, Adrian would've hesitated to bring the animal in. But honestly, this cabin wasn't as nice as most barns back in France.

The mule shuffled forward to sniff the furs, moving toward the woman lying atop them.

She held out a gloved hand and spoke to the animal in English. Then she switched to French. "What's his name?"

Adrien glanced over. "Domino." He picked up the pot from his supplies and headed toward the door.

"Where are you going?"

He paused with his hand on the door latch and turned to look at her. She'd pulled the buffalo robe down as though prepared to launch out of the bed after him. Did she think he planned to walk out the door and not come back?

"Rest easy. I'm gathering snow to melt for water."

Her body seemed to relax into the furs, looking so tiny among them. How long had she been holed up in this cabin without food and warmth?

He turned back to the door and slipped outside. The blizzard still blew with all its fury, slamming into him as he crouched in the snow just beyond the door. He'd left his gloves off to make the work easier, and his numb hands stuck to the cast iron handles on the pot.

With all haste, he slipped back into the cabin, closed the door behind him, then barred it shut against the weather. Domino brayed again, whether to welcome him or protest the gust of wind and snow was hard to tell.

Adrien didn't look at the woman as he worked over the fire, but the burn of her gaze bore into him. Where had she come from? How had she ended up here alone? So many questions, yet they would have to wait until she'd eaten and warmed herself. Maybe then her wariness would ease.

When the snow in the pot melted and grew hot, he scooped out a cup full and turned to the woman. "Drink this to warm you."

She shrank back into the blankets, so he slowed his approach, keeping a little distance between them as he held the mug out.

That seemed to help, for she loosened her clutch on her fur covering and reached for the mug. Her hand trembled, making him hesitate to release the cup into her grasp.

"Here, I'll help hold it while you drink."

Her gaze flew to his face, the wary look turning to full suspicion. What did she think he would do? Dump the hot liquid on her?

He forced his expression to gentle even more. "Just until you get warm. The water is hot, we wouldn't want it to slosh on you."

Her hard expression softened a touch, and she focused on the cup and gripped the handle.

Together, they eased the mug to her lips and she sipped. Her face scrunched as the water went down, probably because of the warmth. The liquid shouldn't be hot enough to scald her, but she must have been frozen through.

Her next swallow was less hesitant, and she started to drink hungrily. When she'd gulped down half the mug, he eased it away.

"Let that settle a bit, then have more."

She sank back onto the pallet, her face more relaxed, lashes sinking lower so her blue eyes were hooded in their shadows. She would probably need a few moments for the hot liquid to work its magic and thaw her from the inside out.

At least she was on her way.

He turned back to the water over the fire, now boiling and ready to accept the venison. Once he got some food into her, he had more than a few questions. Where were they? How had she ended up with no food or warmth?

And the question that loomed strongest in his mind—who was this woman?

Get THIS WILDERNESS JOURNEY at your favorite retailer.

ABOUT THE AUTHOR

 **Misty M. Beller** is a *USA Today* bestselling author of romantic mountain stories, set on the 1800s frontier and woven with the truth of God's love.

Raised on a farm and surrounded by family, Misty developed her love for horses, history, and adventure. These days, her husband and children provide fresh adventure every day, keeping her both grounded and crazy.

Misty's passion is to create inspiring Christian fiction infused with the grandeur of the mountains, writing historical romance that displays God's abundant love through the twists and turns in the lives of her characters.

Sharing her stories with readers is a dream come true for Misty. She writes from her country home in South Carolina and escapes to the mountains any chance she gets.

Connect with Misty at <u>www.MistyMBeller.com</u>

ALSO BY MISTY M. BELLER

Call of the Rockies

Freedom in the Mountain Wind

Hope in the Mountain River

Light in the Mountain Sky

Courage in the Mountain Wilderness

Faith in the Mountain Valley

Honor in the Mountain Refuge

Peace in the Mountain Haven

Calm in the Mountain Storm

Brides of Laurent

A Warrior's Heart

A Healer's Promise

A Daughter's Courage

Hearts of Montana

Hope's Highest Mountain

Love's Mountain Quest

Faith's Mountain Home

Texas Rancher Trilogy

The Rancher Takes a Cook

The Ranger Takes a Bride

The Rancher Takes a Cowgirl

Wyoming Mountain Tales

A Pony Express Romance

A Rocky Mountain Romance

A Sweetwater River Romance

A Mountain Christmas Romance

The Mountain Series

The Lady and the Mountain Man

The Lady and the Mountain Doctor

The Lady and the Mountain Fire

The Lady and the Mountain Promise

The Lady and the Mountain Call

This Treacherous Journey

This Wilderness Journey

This Freedom Journey (novella)

This Courageous Journey

This Homeward Journey

This Daring Journey

This Healing Journey

Made in the USA
Las Vegas, NV
15 May 2023

72115595R00116